WITHDRAWN

MADISON-JEFFERSON COUNTY PUBLIC LIBRARY

GUN-SMOKE

Scorp Plunkett stepped out on the gallery of the Big House and eyed the newcomer appraisingly. The others in the saloon watched on.

A cowboy on a pinto horse was riding down the track.

He was a young man, almost a boy except for his size, and everything he had on spoke of money.

His name was Gun-smoke and he was in a hurry to Las Vegas.

But he hadn't bet on coming across such horse-thieves and sidewinders as those of the Night Riders ...

GUN-SMOKE

Dane Coolidge

MADISON-JEFFERSON COUNTY PUBLIC LIBRARY

This hardback edition 1999
by Chivers Press
by arrangement with
Golden West Literary Agency

Copyright © 1928 by Dane Coolidge
Copyright © 1929 by Dane Coolidge in the
British Commonwealth
Copyright © renewed 1956 by Nancy Collins

All rights reserved

ISBN 0 7540 8077 3

British Library Cataloguing in Publication Data available

Printed and bound in Great Britain by
Redwood Books, Trowbridge, Wiltshire

CONTENTS

CHAPTER	PAGE
I. The Race-track	3
II. Sanctuary	15
III. The Rustler's Daughter	24
IV. Under a Flag	34
V. Like a Piano	46
VI. The Master of Bar C	53
VII. Good Shooting	63
VIII. The Daughter of the Stone-eater	73
IX. Behind the Badge	83
X. The White Wolf	91
XI. Two Lumps of Sugar	100
XII. The Smartest Cowman in Texas	109
XIII. A Horse-trade	116
XIV. A Present for Johnsie	126
XV. The Royal Bengal Tiger	134
XVI. Zim Plunkett Meets His Nemesis	141
XVII. The Queen of the Ball	153

CONTENTS

CHAPTER	PAGE
XVIII. Quick Murrah Eats Dirt	162
XIX. The Duel	169
XX. An Indian Never Forgets	178
XXI. Divided Counsel	185
XXII. The End of the Trail	192
XXIII. In Sunk Valley	198
XXIV. The Bellowing Herd	204
XXV. The Jonahed Shaps	212
XXVI. The Wet Dog	219
XXVII. The Judgment of Watch-eye	224

GUN-SMOKE

GUN-SMOKE

CHAPTER I

THE RACE-TRACK

A LINE of gaunted ponies stood drooping in the sun before the saloon at riotous Portales. There the mountains, stretching wide arms, had enclosed in a broad valley miles and miles of the grassy plains; and at the entrance Scorp Plunkett had built a fence and a gate as a symbol of his power. A huge log, counter-balanced and held down by chain and padlock, blocked the road in front of his house; but to those who rang the bell and asked leave to pass he gave his consent—at a price.

The trail came winding down from the high summit of Horse-thief Pass, worn deep by the feet of many fat steers pushed over the divide at night; but at the head of the broad canyon and from there to Portales, it led off as straight as a race-track. All the pebbles had been picked from this mile-long strip of straight-away, it had been smoothed and made pleasing to the eye; and few there were, with a good horse between their knees, who could keep from testing its speed.

On the gallery of the Big House across the road from the saloon, where Scorp Plunkett dwelt in state, a surly mastiff lay watching the trail; and at a thudding of flying feet he raised his head enquiringly, barked once and glanced at the door. It opened and a long, bony nose was thrust out, then eyes as hard as granite sought out the clatter up the road and Scorp's lips parted in a slow, wolfish smile.

A cowboy on a pinto horse was riding down the track, putting his mount through its paces as he came. He trotted, he single-footed, he broke into a canter; then with a rollicking yelp he jumped his horse into a gallop and set him up with a flourish before the gate. The dogs behind the house came rushing out to bark, the mastiff skinned his teeth and rose up; but not a soul stirred or came out to make him welcome and the stranger reached for the bell.

At its jangle the saloon door showed a flash of staring faces, which disappeared as quickly as they came; then Scorp Plunkett stepped out on the gallery of the Big House and eyed the newcomer appraisingly. He was a young man, almost a boy except for his size, and everything he had on spoke of money. His hat was clear beaver, pressed down over yellow locks which had been spared the shears overlong; his boots were alligator-topped. Bridle and spurs alike were heavy with silver ornaments—only his six-shooter was wooden-handled and plain.

"Hello, thar, Big Boy!" hailed Plunkett, summoning up a jocular smile. "Whar you goin' with that glass-eyed hawse?"

"Down the road, Uncle," answered the stranger genially, "down the road towards the setting sun. So if you'll kindly raise your gate I'll be on my way. Or, if that's too much trouble," he added, "I'll just ask Mister Watch-eye if he can jump it."

At these words the attentive pinto nosed forward and sniffed the gate, then backed up and nodded his head.

"You see?" grinned the cowboy. "He says he can do it." But Plunkett stepped waspishly forth.

"Jest a minute, young man," he said, as the saloon door became suddenly full of heads. "What's yore name, and whar'd you *git* that smart hawse?"

"Name's Gun-Smoke," answered the stranger. "There's my card." And he flipped a big cartridge from his belt.

"Oh, I see," sneered Plunkett, thriftily picking up the cartridge, "you're one of these ba-ad men that's been drifted out of Texas, a jump or two ahead of the sheriff. But you ain't told me whar you got that hawse yet."

"Oh, that's a secret," laughed Gun-smoke, "but he's mine, all right. Ain't you, Watch-eye?" he enquired indulgently.

The pinto, whose glassy eyes seemed always on the watch, nodded his head and arched his neck and Gun-smoke patted him proudly. But Plunkett turned towards the group of hard-looking cowboys and at a signal their leader stepped forth.

He was a tall, swarthy Texan with the still, dark eyes which so often go with Indian blood; and he moved with the agile swiftness of a panther as he strode over and inspected the horse.

"What you think, Quick?" demanded Plunkett significantly. "That hawse ain't got a brand on him."

"Well, that shows," put in Gun-smoke, "that he hasn't been stole. I raised him, myself, from a colt."

"Can he run?" enquired Quick Murrah, with a dubious smile; and Gun-smoke's jovial mood returned.

GUN-SMOKE

"Can you run, Watch-eye?" he asked solicitously and the pinto nodded and pawed the ground.

"Huh! Some trick hawse!" jeered Quick contemptuously. "Never did see a pinto that could run. They're all inbred—got no staying power. Gimme a solid-colored hawse, every time."

For the first time the laughter died out of Gun-smoke's grey eyes but he answered the gunman quietly.

"All right, pardner," he said. "You can have all you want of them, as long as you leave my pinto alone. And now if you gentlemen will step away from that gate I'll hop over it and be on my way."

"What's your hurry?" demanded Quick Murrah insolently. "Having a long-distance race with the sheriff?"

"Is that any of your business?" retorted Gun-smoke belligerently. "You may be out here for your health, yourself."

"I'll make it my business," flashed back Murrah, "if you give me any more lip. But it's the custom with us, when a stranger comes through, he's expected to buy the drinks. Otherwise we turn him back and the sheriff gits him, shore."

He burst out into a hectoring laugh, in which all the others joined, and Gun-smoke saw he was caught.

"All right," he said, swinging down and drooping one rein to the ground; but as he started towards the door of the saloon he saw one of the gang lingering behind. He was a small, wizened-up man whom Gun-smoke had marked from the first; for, half-hidden beneath his grey beard, there was a sinister white line, the mark of a hangman's rope. He was Cutthroat Charley, a horse-thief, driven out of Colorado for his crimes.

THE RACE-TRACK

"Keep away from that horse," warned Gun-smoke. "He looks gentle, but he'll eat you alive."

Then with a last swift glance at Watch-eye, who stood as if nailed to the ground, he led the way to the bar. At his elbow lounged Quick Murrah, a glint of mischief in his eyes as he turned to squint down the line; and his two brothers beyond, both small and swarthy men, answered his wink with knowing smiles. There was something in the wind, perhaps only another sly trick such as they practiced on unwilling guests; but as they drained their glasses Gun-smoke looked them over warily, dropping a bill on the bar as he finished.

"Drink that up, boys," he said, turning quickly towards the door. "I'm due in Las Vegas, right now."

"No! Have one on me!" protested Quick Murrah insistently; but before Gun-smoke could answer there was a yell from outside that made every man whirl about.

"I knew it," grumbled Gun-smoke, and as he hurried out the door he saw Cutthroat Charley on the ground.

"What'd I tell you?" he demanded as the horse-thief looked up; and Cutthroat broke for the door. Behind him, his ears set back, his teeth snapping viciously, the gentle-appearing pinto followed close on his heels, and even Scorp Plunkett laughed.

"The chalk-eyed devil kicked me!" cried Cutthroat as he turned back cursing at the door. "I didn't go near him but he——"

"You're a dadburned liar!" blazed back Gun-smoke. "You tried to steal him, you whelp. Now git—I told you to look out."

GUN-SMOKE

He started towards the horse-thief, and as he turned and fled Gun-smoke whirled and swung up on Watch-eye. In that moment the savage creature had changed to his former self, a gentle, well-trained horse, and Gun-smoke reined him towards the gate.

"I'll pay you fer that!" howled a voice from behind the house; but Gun-smoke only smiled.

"You tell your dog," he said to Plunkett, "if he goes to barking at me I'm liable to ram *this* down his throat— and pull the trigger."

He patted the holster of his wooden-handled pistol but Quick Murrah only laughed.

"Aw, that's Old Charley," he explained. "He's kinder touched in the haid. Ain't never been quite right since they hung him, up at Pueblo, for riding off on another man's hawse. But say, pardner, before you go, that's another custom we have. When a man comes through hyer on a running hawse like yourn we like to match a race."

"Seems to me," complained Gun-smoke, "you folks are full of customs. But Watch-eye ain't no quarter-horse and I can't stop, nohow."

"Yes, you can," broke in a voice from the top of the gate; and Gun-smoke saw that Murrah's brothers had perched themselves on top of it to keep him from attempting the jump.

"You got lots of time," advised Quick. "I reckon we can match you for a half, then."

"No, my horse can't run," protested Gun-smoke. "I'd be glad to accommodate you, but the best he can do is a mile."

THE RACE-TRACK

"A-all right!" agreed Murrah. "Anything for a little excitement. I'll match you for fifty dollars."

"With what?" enquired Gun-smoke cautiously.

"With that little old roan, right out thar in the corral. John, bring up Lightfoot, will ye?"

He turned to his younger brother, who dropped down off the gate, and Gun-smoke ran his eyes over Lightfoot. He was a longlegged, rangy animal, built for speed rather than endurance, and at sight of him Watch-eye snorted and pawed the ground.

"Can you beat him, Old-timer?" enquired Gun-smoke; and Watch-eye nodded violently.

"Come on! I'll bet ye fifty!" urged Quick Murrah.

Gun-smoke looked about at the hard-faced gang of cowboys and scratched his yellow head dubiously.

"Suppose I'd happen to win?" he suggested. "Would you let me go out the gate?"

"Like a bat!" laughed Quick. "And take yore money with you, I don't care if it's a thousand dollars. We'll jest ask Mr. Plunkett, owner of the ZIP outfit, to hold the stakes —all right?"

Gun-smoke surveyed the rugged countenance of Zimiriah Plunkett and nodded assent, though reluctantly. He had heard of the cattle king, whose herds grazed from the Rocky Mountains to the line of the Panhandle in Texas; but, seeing the man himself and the cowboys he had gathered about him, some inner prompting bade him beware.

"Now here," he spoke up. "I'm game to bet on my horse, but it's got to be on the square. If I win I want my money—and I figure on getting it, too—so let's come to an understanding, right away."

"Aw, sho, sho, boy!" spoke up Plunkett. "I reckon you've heerd my name. You leave the stakes with me and you'll git 'em—if you win. These boys is only funnin'!"

"Good enough," agreed Gun-smoke. "I'm full of fun, myself; so I'll raise you to a hundred dollars."

He drew out a roll and Quick Murrah's eyes snapped.

"I'll see you," he mocked, "and raise you a hundred more. You can't run no sandy on me."

Gun-smoke peeled off two bills and handed them over to Zim Plunkett, better known as Old Scorp by his enemies, and Quick Murrah counted out his own. Then, hastily thumbing over the remnant, he placed it in the hands of his boss.

"Thar's two hundred and sixty more," he stated, "if you figger you're due to win."

"I certainly do," responded Gun-smoke, "or I wouldn't bet a cent." And with the battle-lust in his eyes he covered the bet and turned to the staring gang.

"Step up, gentlemen," he said, "if you happen to be feeling lucky. I'll back old Watch-eye up to the last dollar I've got—in the mile."

He counted the rest of his money and after a conference among themselves the ZIP punchers matched it.

"That's a good gun you got thar," suggested Murrah as Gun-smoke stripped down for the race. "How'd you like to put it up against mine?"

He unbelted his ornate six-shooter and passed it over for inspection, but Gun-smoke had already observed it. The

THE RACE-TRACK

head of a longhorned steer was beautifully carved on the mother-of-pearl handle, the guard and lock were inlaid with gold; and yet, for a moment, Gun-smoke hesitated.

"You cain't ride with it, nohow," went on Murrah and impulsively Gun-smoke agreed.

"All right," he grinned. "I'll bet everything I've got—except my horse."

"You bet hawses with me and you'll leave hyar afoot," bantered Quick as he swung up on his mount, "because I'll tell you right now, this nag is a racer. He's never took nobody's dust."

"He'll eat mine," promised Gun-smoke, as he started Watch-eye up the track; and Murrah looked back and laughed. The pistols and the money were in Gun-smoke's big hat, but it was not the custom with the ZIP outfit to let strangers decamp with the loot, especially when they bet their guns. Win or lose, the stakes were as good as his, and he rode rollicking up the course.

"How'll we start?" he asked. "Suit yourself."

"Makes no difference to me," boasted Gun-smoke. "Down at the finish is where I win. Come on—let's whirl and start!"

They were riding neck and neck, a good mile from the gate where Plunkett and his cowboys stood watching; and like the flash of a gun Quick Murrah whirled his roan, leaving Watch-eye twenty feet the first jump. He gained twenty feet more in the next few jumps and although Watch-eye struggled valiantly he was far behind at the quarter-post and further yet at the half. Murrah looked back and whooped hectoringly, the cowboys took up the cheer;

but to stout-hearted Watch-eye the race had just begun and at a word from Gun-smoke he started.

For the first half mile he had run a steady pace while the roan had been fully extended; but now, when Gun-smoke shouted his war-whoop in his ears, the pinto seemed to find his strength. Looking back as he passed the three-quarter post Murrah was astounded to see Watch-eye close behind him. He was running like the wind now, his great nostrils flaring wide as he came hammering down the course; and, grinning confidently through the dust, Gun-smoke was riding like a boy.

With a curse Quick Murrah applied whip and spur at once, the roan jumped and broke its pace; and then with a rush Watch-eye closed up the gap and they were running neck and neck. Murrah was beaten and he knew it, for Lightfoot had shot his bolt, but there was still one tricky chance. Reining his horse over suddenly he hurled its shoulder against the pinto, hoping to knock him from his feet in midair; but the sturdy Watch-eye gave back buffet for buffet and the next moment went thundering past.

The race was won, but at every stride Watch-eye uncorked new sources of speed. With his neck stretched out, his glass eyes gleaming wildly, his feet drumming a victorious tattoo, he came flying down the track towards the disgruntled group of cowboys, while Gun-smoke still urged him on. Behind, eating the dust that the pinto flung back, Lightfoot labored beneath whip and spur; but the heart had gone out of him and he quit before he finished, a good hundred yards from the line.

THE RACE-TRACK

Cowboys scattered right and left as Gun-smoke set up his horse and dropped off before Zimiriah Plunkett.

"All right," he said, "gimme that hatful of money." But Old Scorp held up his hand.

"Jest a minute—jest a minute," he answered. "Mr. Murrah seems to have something on his mind."

"He Navajoed me!" accused Quick, flogging his horse up to the crowd. "Run into me—knocked me plumb off the track. I claim that money on a foul."

"Foul, nothing!" flared back Gun-smoke. "You run into *me*. And I beat you, fair and square."

He reached out to grab the stakes and make his escape, for it was evident he had fallen among thieves, but Zimiriah Plunkett pushed him back.

"Navajo ridin' is barred," he said. "You lose, Mr. Gun-smoke." And he looked up at him with a leering smile.

Gun-smoke glanced about swiftly at the crowd of grinning cowboys, the high gate and his waiting horse. But his pistol was in the hat, along with Quick Murrah's, and he knew now why Murrah had bet it. Yet, guileless as he seemed, Gun-smoke had foreseen this very thing, even before he put up his gun. He had sensed from the start that the gang was out to trick him and he had taken a few precautions of his own. Slipping one hand under the Mexican sash which he had worn for riding he whipped out a short, flat pistol.

"I'll just take those stakes," he stated; and when Plunkett jerked back he slammed him over the head with his gun. Then with one swift grab he snatched up both the six-shooters, throwing his pocket pistol into the dirt.

GUN-SMOKE

"How about it?" he enquired, turning their muzzles on the gang; and the cowboys stood rooted to the spot.

Gun-smoke thrust the two guns into the slack of his waistband while he slung the two belts over one arm. Then ramming his hat, money and all, firmly down on his head he swung up on Watch-eye and faced them.

"The first yap that shoots I'll shore git 'im!" he warned, and turned the dancing Watch-eye towards the gate.

He bounded towards it in crouching leaps, gathering speed as he approached, and plunged over it as lightly as a bird. Gun-smoke turned, gun in hand, but the cowboys had had enough—already they were running for the house.

"Ah-hah, hah!" he laughed, "hunt your holes, you danged prairie-dogs!" And with a whoop he galloped away.

CHAPTER II

Sanctuary

GUN-SMOKE'S hat was full of money, he was over Scorp Plunkett's gate and the road lay open to the south; but as he galloped away Watch-eye shied at a low bush, almost throwing his rider to the ground. Gun-smoke rose up, clutching the horn, and over the top of the bush he caught the sinister gleam of a gun; then something struck his leg, knocking his boot from the stirrup, and he grabbed for the horn again. Some assassin, lying in wait, had shot him from ambush, but his leg seemed as good as before.

Gun-smoke rose up in the saddle and, crouching behind the bush, he saw Cutthroat Charley, the horse-thief. His pistol was still smoking and as he looked it spat again—then Gun-smoke fired twice and the horse-thief went sprawling, flapping his arm like a wing-broken bird. He leapt up and grabbed his gun again as if preparing to shoot left-handed and Gun-smoke swung low and rode.

Back at Portales he could see the gang running out with their rifles, there was the whine of bullets going past; but Watch-eye never faltered and Gun-smoke rose up laughing as the last of the rifle-shots ceased. The gate had been thrown open and horse after horse came galloping in his wake.

GUN-SMOKE

Gun-smoke reached down and patted Watch-eye on the neck and he fell into a long, easy lope.

"Stay with it, boy," he said, "they can't ketch you and I know it. We'll show that bunch of hounds they can't ride or shoot or nothing! And come sundown we'll lose 'em, to boot."

He glanced up at the sun, which had descended in the west until it almost touched the top of the mountains. In an hour it would be down and as darkness mantled the plains he could circle and throw off his pursuers. They came on now in a compact body instead of strung out down the road, and though at the end of every mile they were further and further behind they did not abandon the chase. Gun-smoke had never heard of Zim Plunkett's Night Riders, who scoured the plains to wipe out his enemies, but there was something about their confidence which somehow dashed his spirits and he searched the rugged canyons as he passed.

Each was formed like the gateway at treacherous Portales —a narrow opening between low cliffs, then a broad, enclosed park and beyond, the shadowy ridges of the heights. Trampled cow-trails led up the washes that meandered out across the plains to be lost in the coulees below; but the main road led south, skirting the edge of the hills, and Gun-smoke held resolutely on. For what had he to fear, with Watch-eye between his knees? On the trail he was tireless as an antelope.

The sun set in splendor behind the jagged peaks but as Gun-smoke scanned the heights a sudden weakness came over him, his brain whirled and he felt himself swaying.

SANCTUARY

He recovered himself instantly, then with growing alarm he ran his hand down inside his left boot. In the chase he had barely noticed the bullet-hole through his boot-top, the sting which had turned to an ache; but as he felt the warm wetness his senses reeled again—he was hit, his boot was full of blood.

Gun-smoke came to clutching the pommel, the faithful Watch-eye swaying under him to keep him from falling to the ground; and as he saw in the distance the bobbing heads of his pursuers he held fast and urged his horse to a gallop. If he halted by the wayside he would be beaten and robbed, perhaps killed by the vengeful riders. It was necessary to quit the road and seek out a hiding-place where he could rest and bind up his wound.

An open trail appeared before him, leading off up a canyon, and he took it on the run, regardless. Then a fence appeared before him, across the neck of the entrance, and he braced himself for the jump. Watch-eye hesitated, for he was tired, then bounded nimbly over it, his hoofs hitting the upper bar as he passed. They were in a pasture now, where a stream ran down through the willows, and though the shadows were gathering fast Gun-smoke could see a slab cabin, set back against the slope of the hill.

He reined towards it and shut his eyes, holding fast with both hands, but as he came up at a lope there was a sharp challenge from the doorway, a woman's scream and the flash of a gun. It blazed out in his very face and at the roar Watch-eye shied, then with a heart-breaking thump Gun-smoke landed on his head and the world became a blank.

It was light when he came to and soft, unfamiliar hands were brushing the matted hair from his eyes. He stirred and went out again and at last, far away, he heard a woman's voice—she was crying.

"What's the matter?" he muttered and suddenly two scalding tears splashed down on his grimy cheek.

"Are you dead?" a small voice faltered and he looked up quickly, then moaned and closed his eyes. Above him there hovered a face such as he had seen in pictures of angels, a woman with broad brows and an aureole of dark hair, and her brown eyes were infinitely sad. Perhaps he *was* dead and this fairest of all angels was ministering to his needs. He moved his dry lips and whispered for water and a cool gourd was pressed to his mouth. He drank then, slowly, rolling his eyes as he looked around, and sank back with a sigh. Everything that he saw was strange and a great weariness held him in its thrall.

"I—I thought you were dead," spoke up the tragic voice again and Gun-smoke summoned a smile.

"Nope," he answered. "Thought I heard the angels singing but——"

The frightened face moved closer, her fragrant hair brushed his cheek and suddenly the angel smiled.

"Then you're going to get well," she said; and Gun-smoke felt water on his brow. His head seemed big and very sore, and the sting of open wounds suddenly roused him.

"Say, where am I?" he demanded, trying in vain to sit up; but she pressed him back on the bed. He was inside a cabin, made of hewn stakes set side by side, and the girl

SANCTUARY

who leaned over him, searching for wounds on his bloody head, was not an angel at all. She was frowning now, though her eyes were still tearful as she tore open his shirt and scanned his chest.

"You're in Heck Blood's cabin," she answered vindictively, "and I shot you—why didn't you stop?"

"Search me," grumbled Gun-smoke. "Who the hell is Heck Blood? I don't remember this place."

"Well, Heck Blood," she informed him, "is the man you came to kill. But my daddy had gone to town and I got you in the door—I can't find that bullet-hole anywhere."

"It's in my leg," protested Gun-smoke. "What you want to shoot me for? I was hurt, and I came here for help."

"Which leg?" she demanded and when she jerked off his left boot she gave a cry and sank to the floor. "Oh, I've killed him!" she moaned. "But why didn't you stop? Your boot is full of blood!"

"Never mind," mumbled Gun-smoke. "Tie a rag around the hole. And say, what'd you do with my horse?"

He sat up quickly, his eyes rolling wildly, but she pushed him resolutely back.

"You lie still," she ordered, "if you don't want to die." And gazing at him sternly she opened up his bloody wound and bound it tight with a cloth. "Now," she said, "who are you, anyway? And what are you doing up our canyon?"

"Name's Gun-smoke," he stated. "I got shot, back at Portales, and come up here for help."

"Got shot!" she repeated, looking him over in dismay. "What—again? Oh, now I know he'll die!"

GUN-SMOKE

"Something hit me in the head," he responded dully. "But say, I want my horse!"

She felt his head over anxiously, then stepped to the door as the hounds bayed a fresh alarm.

"Somebody's coming," she announced. "Down at the gate."

"It's them ZIP cowboys," he said. "I remember now—they chased me down the road. Then I turned off up this canyon—but say, can you see my horse?"

"He's right out there," she answered. "Aren't you one of Scorp's Night Riders? I took you in the dark for Quick Murrah!"

"No!" he burst out peevishly; but with a quick triumphant movement she dangled an ornate pistol before his eyes.

"Where'd you get this gun, then?" she demanded. "That belongs to Quick Murrah, and I know it!"

"I won it in a horse-race," he replied and she tossed her head, smiling dubiously.

"And I suppose," she went on, "you won this hatful of money, too? Not that *I* care!" she ended defiantly.

"Sure I won it," he cried. "But they wouldn't give it up. So I hit Scorp over the head and took it away from him. Then I jumped over the gate and was making a getaway when some feller shot me from the brush."

"You lie down," she ordered, laying a hand on his brow; but Gun-smoke was not to be denied.

"No!" he insisted, "I want my horse in here. Them fellers will steal him, and then I'll have to kill them. Open the door and he'll come right up."

SANCTUARY

He put his finger inside his mouth and gave a long, shrill whistle and the next minute there was a thud outside the door. The girl peered out the key-hole, her face set in disbelief, then she sprang to a loop-hole and looked out.

"They're coming," she said in a hushed voice. "It's the Night Riders, to burn our cabin."

"Well, let my horse in," he clamored, "and I'll whip the whole shooting-match for you. Here, Watch-eye! Now—open the door!"

For a moment she hesitated, then at a snort by the key-hole she snatched open the door and stepped back. Like a soldier under orders Watch-eye paced soberly in and she slammed the door behind him and grabbed her gun. It was a huge, repeating rifle but she thrust it out the loop-hole just as the horsemen came galloping up.

"Hello, thar!" hailed a voice and the girl turned and whipped out the light.

"Hello, yourse'f!" she answered back defiantly, "and don't you come no nearer! I know you, Quick Murrah, so look out!"

"Aw, sho, sho, Johnsie!" appealed Murrah from the darkness, "we ain't come to burn down yore house. We're after a hawse-thief and we're going to git him, too, so you might as well open up."

"You keep away!" she shrilled, "or I'll fill you full of lead! And when my daddy comes back he'll sure make you hard to ketch if you try any foolishness with *me!*"

She pulled back the hammer and at the click of the lock there was a startled silence outside.

GUN-SMOKE

"All we want is that man," spoke up a placating voice. "We seen him go in thar, Johnsie."

"You did not!" she replied. "And you can't have him, anyway, I don't care if he is a horse-thief."

"And we want that hawse," added Murrah.

"You tell him to go to hell!" admonished Gun-smoke from the bed, but Johnsie answered never a word.

"He's a bad man from Texas," went on Murrah after a pause. "Done shot one of the boys up at Portales and hit old Zim over the haid."

"Good for him!" applauded Johnsie. "I hope he kills all of you."

"Ain't liable to," responded Quick, "because we aim to string him up. He robbed Mr. Plunkett of a whole hatful of money and rode off on his black pinto hawse."

Johnsie glanced over at Watch-eye, who was black with white markings, but she kept her gun out the loop-hole.

"We seen you lead his hawse in," ended Murrah, "so you might as well give him up."

Gun-smoke woke up suddenly to the fate which was in store for him if this woman yielded to their demands. He would be hung for a horse-thief, strung up to some tree by Quick Murrah and his lawless gang, and yet he was too weak to move. On his bed lay the pistol he had taken from Murrah, but his hand was too weak to lift it, even when he summoned all his strength. He fell back, half-fainting, and like a man in a dream he heard the angel-voice speak.

"You git out of heah!" she cried in the softest of Southern accent, "or I'll shoot every one of you—you cowards! This man is in our house, and what would Daddy say if he heard I'd given him up?"

Gun-smoke drifted away then into a land where ghostly voices came dimly to his ears; but the sweetest voice of all had a soft, Virginia accent and he knew that one angel was his friend.

CHAPTER III

THE RUSTLER'S DAUGHTER

GUN-SMOKE was roused from his faint by a low snort in his ear, the anxious nudge of a velvety nose. It was Watch-eye, standing over his bed. In the light of a tallow dip Johnsie Blood regarded them curiously, her hair thrown back, her hands leaning on the gun which had made the dreaded Night Riders retreat.

"Hello, Watch-eye," he muttered, and at the sound of his master's voice the pinto whickered and shook his head joyously.

"He seems to like you," spoke up Johnsie and Gun-smoke stroked his nose.

"Bet y'r life," he murmured. "We're pardners."

"Quick Murrah claims you stole him," she said; but Gun-smoke only grunted.

"Keep away from him," he warned, "he's a one-man horse. If you touch him he'll eat you alive."

"Oh, no," she laughed, "he wouldn't bite me." And she laid a small hand on his neck.

Watch-eye threw back his ears and his glassy eyes gleamed wickedly but Gun-smoke spoke sharply from the bed.

"Watch!" he commanded, "don't you bite the lady. She's our friend, and a danged good friend.—You'd better go away," he added.

THE RUSTLER'S DAUGHTER

"Not much!" answered Johnsie, her hand still on Watch-eye's neck; and while he snorted and snapped his teeth she patted his neck. "Now *you* go away," she ordered, and Watch-eye reluctantly obeyed.

"He's been standing there," she smiled, "ever since I lit the candle—but I've got to find that other bullet-hole."

She flexed his arms experimentally, then examined his broad chest and felt of his other leg.

"Where does it hurt?" she questioned, anxiously.

"It's my haid!" he insisted and she burst out laughing.

"I reckon you're from Texas," she said.

"Of co'se I am," he answered, "but how did *you* know?"

"When you talked about your 'haid'," she mimicked. "I've heard 'em say," she went on, as she felt his bruised scalp, "that you Texans can't be hurt in those parts, and now I surely believe it. Because I'd swear that's where I shot you."

"Maybe your shooting isn't so good," he suggested maliciously. "I've seen girls that couldn't hit nothing."

"Don't you worry about my shooting," she retorted. "I noticed that Quick Murrah and that gang of Night Riders were glad to let me alone. But say, I believe you're going to recover—you're able to talk back to your nurse."

"Heh, heh—yes," mocked Gun-smoke, "and I know where *you* come from, too. I can tell by the way you say 'about'!"

"Well, where *am* I from?" she answered tartly. "That is, if it's any of your business."

"You're from Virginia," he stated confidently. "That is, if you're not one of these F.F.Vs from Missouri."

"Now you quit mocking me," she warned, "or I'll put your old horse out, and make you lie down and keep still.

But I might as well tell you we *are* one of the First Families and we're not from Missouri, either."

"Just water-bound in Arkansaw for a couple of years, eh?" he jested and she laughed as she shook her head.

"No," she said, "we're from Texas ourselves; but my Dad is one Texan that won't admit it. The worse they are, it seems, the prouder they are of it—look at old Zim Plunkett and Quick Murrah!"

"That's a hard outfit," admitted Gun-smoke. "If it hadn't been for my horse I'd never got away from there alive. But old Watch-eye took one jump and crow-hopped over that gate—and me with all their money, and everything."

"Yes, and Quick Murrah says you done *stole* that horse," she repeated; but Gun-smoke pretended not to hear.

"First they made me buy the drinks," he ran on garrulously, "and then they tried to rib up a horse-race. But nope, there was nothing doing—I told 'em Mister Watch-eye couldn't run, except a mile. Well, all right, they'd run me a mile then; and when we got through betting all our money was in my hat. Then I put up my six-shooter against Quick's little piece of jewelry and Old Scorp held the pot.

"But I knowed all the time they were figuring to rob me so I tucked a little pocket-gun right down inside my belt here—and sure enough, they claimed a foul. I just tapped old Zim over the coco with my pistol, grabbed the stakes and swung up on my horse. And the next minute old Watch-eye was plumb over the gate and running like a bat out of hell. I'd've made a clean git-away, only that feller with the cut neck laid in wait for me and plugged me from behind."

"Do you expect me to believe all that?" she enquired

THE RUSTLER'S DAUGHTER

sarcastically. "Then you lie down, while I bathe your 'haid.' Because I know very well you couldn't jump their gate—and Quick claims you *stole* that horse."

"All right," returned Gun-smoke, turning ugly, "you show me the man that can lay a hand on Watch and I'll make him a present of the horse. But until then I don't make no apologies to nobody—you're *my* horse, ain't you Watch?"

Watch-eye came over promptly and laid his head on Gun-smoke's shoulder and Johnsie almost believed him.

"Well, all right," she challenged, "what's your name, then? I know it isn't Gun-smoke."

"You wait till I get well and go back to Portales—I'll show 'em if that ain't my name!"

"Yes, but you won't show me," she reminded him; but Gun-smoke did not seem to care. He moved about uneasily and glanced around the room, then coughed and came to the point.

"Excuse me for mentioning it," he said, "but I haven't had anything to eat since yesterday. And losing that bootful of blood has sure left me hongry. Have you got a little something you can spare?"

"Why, sure!" she answered quickly, and then she checked herself. "That is," she qualified, "if you don't mind beef straight—we haven't got a thing in the house."

"Oh, that's all right," agreed Gun-smoke with another glance at the barren room. "I could eat a roast mule, stuffed with fire-crackers."

She smiled at him half-heartedly and hurried into the other room, where he heard her fanning up a blaze.

"You see," she apologized, "Dad has got lots of enemies

and—he doesn't go to town very often. But today he took mother and they went down to Barcee. Zim Plunkett is trying to move us."

"What for?" demanded Gun-smoke, after a silence.

"Oh—because he doesn't like us," she answered evasively. "We had trouble with him, back in Texas."

"That old wolf is sure bad—and he's going to come to a bad end," predicted Gun-smoke as he listened to the popping of grease. "Is that some of his beef you're cooking?"

"Sure is!" she responded easily. "Dad won't eat any other kind. He says it doesn't taste the same."

"Uh-huh!" grunted Gun-smoke and nodded his head sagely. So Heck Blood was a rustler and his dark-eyed daughter had been raised on company beef. He sighed, for only a short time before he had thought that Johnsie was an angel. True, she had received him as rustlers' daughters were likely to do, with the whang of a gun when he charged; but she had more than made up for that trifling discourtesy by the way she had stood off Quick Murrah. She was the fighting child of a fighting sire, and pulling yearlings from Old Scorp was hardly in the category of stealing. It was almost commendable, considering the circumstances—and yet he sighed again.

Like all true cowmen he had an aversion to petty larceny and the small-scale pilferings of nesters. It was the resort of sordid minds, untuned to the high emprise which builds up big herds with the running-iron. To ride forth on the range and brand mavericks and *orejanos* smacked of the days when cattlemen were kings, but to come down in some canyon and kill a cow at a time for beef was too much like common stealing. But while he sighed for her Johnsie was sighing for him—because Gun-smoke is not a man's name.

"Here it is," she announced as she brought in a broad platter; but as Gun-smoke wolfed down the meat she regarded him sadly, for he did not look like a horse-thief. His brow was too high and wide, his bruised features clean-cut and regular; and there was a look in his eyes that stirred something within her, a dim longing to protect him from harm.

"Where'd you come from?" she asked at last; and he gave her an impish grin.

"Where do all cow-thieves come from?" he parried.

"What do you mean?" she flared up fiercely. "Are you hinting that my Dad's a cow-thief? He never did a crooked or dishonorable thing in his life—these cattle that he takes are his!"

"How do you mean?" enquired Gun-smoke, working away at the juicy steak. "You mean they're his when he gits them?"

"No, they're his already!" she stormed. "Zim Plunkett stole them from him!"

"I see," smiled Gun-smoke, "he's just stealing them back again." And she gave him a look to smite him dead.

"A man in your line of business," she said at last, "and travelling under a flag to boot, ought to pick and choose his words a little more. My Dad is a gentleman, I'll have you to understand, and he never stole anything—ever!"

"My mistake," bowed Gun-smoke, "I stand corrected, Madame. Proceed, and let's get this thing straight."

"You think you're smart, don't you?" she commented

acidly. "But I'll tell you, all the same. My folks moved from Virginia after the war, but Dad had a little trouble out in Kansas when Quantrell's guerillas got after him. So we moved down into Texas and Dad had lots of cows, only nobody would come and buy them. We just couldn't find a market, at any price. Well, it was three years ago that Zim Plunkett came through the country, hunting up old Confederate soldiers and buying their cattle, cheap. Dad had been a soldier, too—he was a Colonel under Lee—and when Plunkett came to the house and said he'd served the Confederacy why naturally there was nothing too good for him.

"Poor Dad," she sighed, "he'll never make a business man —he puts too much trust in strangers. Anyway he sold Old Scorp two thousand head of cattle and took his note, for ten dollars a head; and what does Plunkett do but move them up to the Panhandle and then across the line into New Mexico! He bought cattle from everybody—forty-five or fifty thousand—and now he won't pay the notes."

"Why not?" demanded Gun-smoke innocently.

"Why, because the notes are outlawed! He's moved out of the state of Texas. And he intended to do it, all the time!"

"I see," nodded Gun-smoke. "You can't collect."

"That's just what we're doing!" she stated savagely. "And it makes me so mad when some stranger, like you, says my father is stealing beef. These steers that he kills have got his own brand on them—he sold them, but they never were paid for—and I'd just like to ask you if you consider that stealing? Well, of course not! He's taking his own!"

THE RUSTLER'S DAUGHTER

"Why, sure!" shrilled Gun-smoke. "More power to his elbow! I'd like nothing better than to take on as a cowhand and run off a few, myself."

"And we settled right here," continued Johnsie vindictively, "although Dad just hates a nester. But we've been here for two years and Quick Murrah and all the rest of them can't make us move—not an inch! They've murdered those poor homesteaders and ran off their stock and burned down their cabins by the hundred; but they can't move my Dad, because he knows he is right! And what's more, he's a fighting Blood!"

She nodded her head vigorously and Gun-smoke glanced at her quizzically.

"And I reckon," he added, "you're a fighting Blood your ownself. Well, there ain't any Colonels in my family, but I'm a first-class fighting-man, myself."

"Either that or a first-class liar!" she answered and then she broke down and laughed.

"Well, there's no use pretending," she said. "We've stuck here, but we haven't enjoyed it. And Old Scorp will get us, yet. We're the only homesteaders that have settled on his range that the Night Riders haven't moved. But we're trying to hold on until the railroad comes through, and maybe that will tame things down."

She sighed and turned away to peer out through the loop-hole and Gun-smoke gazed at her in silence. She was not the kind of woman that was found in two-roomed cabins, with gun-holes under the eaves. There was something indeed very appealing and feminine in this daughter of bold Colonel Blood.

GUN-SMOKE

"Say," he said at last, "if there's anything that I can do for you don't hesitate to say the word. And if those Night Riders come back you just help me outside the door and I'll smoke 'em up with these."

He patted the two six-shooters but she only smiled wryly.

"I don't need any help," she said. "I just hate that Quick Murrah, and if I ever get a bead on him—that's how I came to shoot you. But when I turned you over and saw it wasn't Quick I—I couldn't help it—I cried."

"You sure did me a good turn," he nodded, "when you saved me from that bunch of killers. They'd've plugged me in a minute if I'd fell by the road—that's why I turned up your canyon."

"I—I'm glad you came, anyway," she stammered at last. "It gets kind of lonely, sometimes."

"Well, I'm gladder than you are," he answered, noting the blush that crept to her brow. "Because I might have rode by here and never knowed you were in the world."

She glanced at him shyly, then turned back to her loophole and Gun-smoke bit his lip. Something told him that if he talked he was more than likely to say something which on the morrow he would bitterly regret. But she was really such a wonderful girl. And as he watched her he wondered if, after all, the words were better unsaid.

There was a shot from down the canyon, then the rattle of pistol-fire and a terrific baying of hounds.

"Oh, they're trying to kill Daddy!" she screamed and Gun-smoke grabbed for his gun.

"Pack me out there!" he shouted, "where I can get

a clean shot at them. I'll watch your cabin—you jump up on Watch-eye and ride down and give 'em hell!"

"No! They're coming!" she replied. "You stay where you are—I can tend to those cowards alone!"

He listened and above the chorus of baying hounds he could hear the rush of galloping hoofs. But just as he heaved up and went hobbling towards the door she leapt down and snatched him back.

"It's Daddy!" she cried. "Can't you hear him cuss?" And Gun-smoke dropped back on his bed.

CHAPTER IV

Under a Flag

THE cursing of Colonel Blood, which was of the frontier variety, was brought to a sudden stop by the appearance of his daughter, who bounded out the door into his arms.

"Hello, Daddy!" she cried. "I'm all right. Hello, Mother, did you bring the things? And oh, Quick Murrah was here. They were chasing a horse-thief!" she whispered. "And he's right inside!" she added.

"A hawse-thief?" repeated the Colonel in a voice that shook the timbers, and the next moment he strode through the door.

"Well, by the Almighty!" he thundered as he saw Gun-smoke reclining on his bed. "It seems to me, for a total stranger, he's making himse'f strictly at home. And what the devil is this? Has he moved in, hawse and all?" And he stood staring at the nonchalant Watch-eye.

"Keep away from that horse," warned Gun-smoke, belligerently, "or he's liable to take an arm off. And if I ain't welcome, I'll sure make myself scarce—I don't let no man call me a horse-thief!"

He faced the bearded Colonel, whose bleak, stone-grey eyes were fixed on him with arrogant scorn; but before her father could speak Johnsie flung herself between them and came to Gun-smoke's defense.

"That's just what Quick Murrah called him, when he wanted to string him up. But I told him you'd never forgive me if I gave up a man that was our guest."

"Certainly not!" asserted the Colonel, "but how come he's a guest heah? Did you invite him into our house?"

"No. I—I shot him! But I thought it was Quick Murrah! And then—can't you see—I was sorry!"

"Why, yes, yes, my little dove," soothed Blood, patting her head. "I'm very sorry if the gentleman is hurt. But what was he doing heah to make it necessary to shoot him? Now tell me the truth!" And he smiled.

"Well, he claims," she faltered, "that he got in a fight at Portales and they shot him in the leg when he left. And when he was riding by he got weak—and they were after him. So he turned off up our canyon. But I didn't know that and when he rode up charging I shot him, but I didn't mean to."

"You never shot me at all!" protested Gun-smoke stoutly. "I got this leg up at Portales. And since the fire-works are all over and nobody hurt I'll just bid you one and all—good-bye!"

He hobbled over towards his horse, his eyes blinking angrily, but the Colonel waved him back.

"Never mind, young man," he said, "you are welcome to remain heah. But that hawse will have to go."

"If he goes, I go!" answered Gun-smoke defiantly. "I don't want Quick Murrah to get him."

"Is it necessary," demanded Blood, "to turn my house

into a stable? Heah's my wife, suh, and my daughter——"

Gun-smoke bowed to Mrs. Blood, who met his glance with a quick smile; and bowed again, but sulkily, to Johnsie; but as he took Watch-eye by the bridle and started for the door the women both spoke up at once.

"Very well," assented the Colonel with a snort, "the law of hospitality is sacred. You can keep your hawse, young man, any place you dam' please, as long as my women-folks are satisfied."

He glanced at his wife, a small woman with soft brown eyes and a tired but appealing smile, and she patted his hand approvingly.

"We are sorry," she said, "that our accommodations are so meager, but you are very welcome, Mister——"

"Er—Gun-smoke," replied the stranger and after a startled glance at her husband Mrs. Blood extended her hand. Gun-smoke bowed and shook hands in silence, then turned his sullen eyes to the man who had called him a horse-thief. The Colonel blinked, then gravely offered his hand while he murmured welcoming words.

"My daughter," he added. "Mistuh—er—Gun-smoke. I judge you're already acquainted."

"Yes, sir," he responded; but Johnsie came bravely forward and offered her lily-white hand.

"You'd better lie down," she suggested, and pointed to fresh blood on the floor.

"Just throw me down a robe," objected Gun-smoke. "I don't want to occupy your bed."

"No, suh," protested Blood, suddenly recovering his poise, "our bed is none too good for a guest, and especially for one who is hurt." And drawing Gun-smoke's arm over his shoulder he helped him back to the couch.

It was made of rawhide thongs, stretched tight over a hewn frame; but as Gun-smoke sank back it seemed like a bed of down, and already Mrs. Blood had taken charge. Heating water over the fire she washed the throbbing wound, where the bullet had passed through his leg, and before Gun-smoke knew it he had sunk into a slumber from which he did not awaken until dawn. Then as he opened his eyes he saw the proud Colonel wrapped up in a blanket on the floor; and in the corner, whickering softly, he beheld patient Watch-eye, who was waiting for his master to get up.

Gun-smoke lay knitting his brows, gazing first at the Colonel and then at his horse, in the house; and when by degrees the events of the evening came back to him he straightened up and examined his leg. But for it he would have slipped away quietly, but it was swollen and stiff in the joint. The bullet had passed through the outside of the calf, leaving a clean hole at either side, and as he felt of it he saw the Colonel watching him.

"Good morning, suh," he greeted, "I hope you passed a restful night. That's a bad leg you've got theah, and you'll have to keep off of it, but Mrs. Blood will attend to your wants."

"Thank you, Colonel," replied Gun-smoke. "Sorry to make you any trouble——"

"No trouble—no trouble at all, suh! We are delighted to have your company. And anything I can do for yourse'f or your hawse——"

"Well, just open that door, then," suggested Gun-smoke

GUN-SMOKE

with a guilty grin. "Because it's about time old Watch-eye went out."

"Out he goes, then," observed Colonel Blood grimly, as he rose up and stamped on his boots; and when the door was thrown open Watch-eye paced decorously out and trotted down to the creek for a drink.

"And now," went on the Colonel, producing a bottle from the pack which he had brought back from the store, "how would you like a little toddy, befoah breakfast?"

He brought hot water from the kitchen, where the womenfolks were astir, and as Gun-smoke sipped the liquor and sniffed the fragrance of coffee and bacon he sighed and settled back on his bed. Since he was destined to nurse his wound for several days, he had made, it seemed, a very happy choice, not only of his hostess but his host. He had fallen, in fact, into an atmosphere so congenial that, after breakfast was served and his leg freshly dressed, he had only one regret.

Since she had glanced in through the doorway and bade him a polite good morning the girl of his dreams, the fair Johnsie, had carefully kept away from him.

Some great preparations were afoot for she was hurrying to and fro in the other room. Trunks were opened and dresses shaken out, he caught a glimpse of a new ribbon binding up her wealth of hair; but Johnsie herself, who had been so friendly and approachable, was suddenly and unaccountably shy. He heard the click of high-heeled slippers on the puncheon floor, the swish of a trailing gown, and at the vision of loveliness that flitted across the doorway he went dizzy and closed his eyes. She was a queen now in her young beauty, and on her lips there was a smile that revealed a hidden dimple in each cheek. But she did not come in to exhibit her pretty dress, and Gun-smoke fell to wondering again.

Had he, on the evening before, made some remarks in her presence which had offended this capricious queen? Or had her parents forbidden her to associate with one who was reputed to be a horse-thief? He lay gazing out the doorway at the hillside beyond, where Watch-eye was cropping the grama-grass as free and untrammelled as a deer. Perhaps his insistence on keeping his horse inside the house had had something to do with this frost. Perhaps—he was still speculating when the Colonel came in, bringing his hat, which had disappeared over night.

"Heah's your hat, Mistuh—ah—Gun-smoke," he said. "I trust you will find all your money," he added; and Gun-smoke laughed uneasily.

"Oh—yes," he said, as he pawed it over carelessly and spread it out on the bed. "I left Portales in a hurry after that horse-race—never stopped to take it out of my hat."

He counted it over and, as he stored it in his pockets, he felt the Colonel's stern eyes upon him. It was upwards of a thousand dollars.

"My daughter informs me," he said at last, "that you had trouble with Zim Plunkett at Portales. Did he win your money in a hawse-race?"

"No—*sir!*" grinned Gun-smoke. "I won *his* money."

"With that hawse?" enquired Blood incredulously.

"You bet ye!" nodded Gun-smoke. "But they tried to beat me out of it. That's a hard outfit, if I'm any judge."

GUN-SMOKE

"That's correct," stated the Colonel, "but—er—what hawse did you run against? Their nag, Lightfoot, has never been beaten."

"He was beaten yesterday," asserted Gun-smoke, "and here's the money to prove it. And Quick Murrah's six-shooter, to boot."

He drew the ornate pistol from under a fold in his blanket and the Colonel's eyes gleamed as he examined it.

"That's his gun," he agreed, "but you'll excuse me if I doubt it—your pinto never beat Quick's Lightfoot. Theah's only one hawse, suh, in this part of the country, that is even considered his equal and that's Dandy McAllister's Bird-Catcher."

"No, doubt it all you want to," answered Gun-smoke flaring up. "My old man told me when I started for this country not to try to show you wise hombres anything—and especially about horse-racing and shooting."

"Of co'se," qualified the Colonel. "I don't wish to doubt your word. But in Virginia, suh, I was considered a judge of hawse-flesh and your pinto doesn't look like a quarter-hawse."

"He isn't," agreed Gun-smoke, "and that's what I told them. So, just for a little excitement, Mr. Murrah ran me a mile."

"And you beat him!" whooped Colonel Blood, slapping Gun-smoke on the back. "I ask your pardon a thousand times, suh! And did you win his pistol, to boot? Young man, you've been wasted on wherever you came from—we need you, right heah, in this country!"

"I believe it," grinned Gun-smoke as the Colonel poured

out two tall drinks and held his glass on high. "But I'm due in Las Vegas, right now."

"And is it possible?" demanded the Colonel, "that you jumped your hawse over their gate and escaped from that deadfall with the stakes?"

"There's my winnings," answered Gun-smoke. "And you saw the way they chased me. What's the matter—did you think I was lying?"

"No, no!" protested Blood, "I never doubt the word of a gentleman. But Johnsie rather thought that the blow on your head——"

"I see," nodded Gun-smoke. "But I was just going to tell you, I never told a lie in my life. It's a matter of principle—that's why I get bowed up when anybody doubts my word."

He glanced at the door, where Johnsie stood listening, and she pouted and drew away; but the Colonel only smiled.

"You'll do," he observed, "but what pleases me most was your hitting Old Scorp over the head. Theah's the most unprincipled scoundrel in the Territory of New Mexico. He makes a business of fleecing strangers when they come over that trail, and when he isn't abusing settlers and driving them off his range he's stealing cattle from Dandy McAllister.

"You have heard, of co'se," went on the Colonel, leaning back and lighting a cigar, "of Mistah McAllister, of Barcee? He's the gentleman who gave me these cigahs. I was personally acquainted with his family, back in Virginia, but his father married a No'therner. She came from a good family, but the alliance was unfortunate—they finally parted and Dandy's father came out heah to engage in the cattle industry. He was killed only a short time ago, and young Dandy has taken over the ranch."

He puffed thoughtfully on his cigar and as Gun-smoke meditated on young McAllister's generosity Blood grunted and knocked off the ash.

"Dandy's a very fine fellow," he observed judicially. "I like him—he's generous to a fault. But if he has a failing he lacks the fighting blood that all the McAllisters were proud of. I ascribe that, Mistuh—ah—Gun-smoke, to his mother. She was one of these No'therners—a very estimable lady, but not fitted to raise a son. So if Dandy has a failing it's in letting Zim Plunkett steal his cattle.

"It's against my principles, suh, to allow any man to dictate to me or tell me what to do or not to do. I fought on both sides during the late misunderstanding—first as a colonel under Lee and then as a bush whacker against Quantrell when his guerillas invaded Kansas. In both cases I was defeated but no man can say that Heck Blood ever compromised with principle. I am a firm believer, suh, in the rights of the individual; and Zim Plunkett and all his men can never drive me from this canyon, and steal my cattle unpunished."

"Oh, but Daddy," protested Johnsie, who had come back to the doorway. "I don't think you're quite fair to Dandy."

"Perhaps not," returned the Colonel, with a wave of his hand, "but run on about your duties, my daughter. As I said before, McAllister is a gentleman, and generous to a fault; but it makes my blood boil to see that trifling scoundrel, Plunkett, systematically running off his stock."

UNDER A FLAG

"But if Dandy would offer to fight him, Quick Murrah and all his gang——"

"Don't mention the name of that rascal in my presence!" stormed the Colonel, turning upon his daughter; and when she had fled from her father's wrath he spoke on in a half-whisper to Gun-smoke. "I have warned him from my home," he said, "and if I find him heah I'll kill him like a dog. He has had the effrontery to presume to co'te my daughter—and him nothing but a half-Indian cow-thief."

"He's a bad one," observed Gun-smoke impersonally

"But with me, suh," went on the Colonel, "it is family that counts. I don't care what you say, blood counts in hawses and men; and the curse of this country is these low-flung renegades that try to rule by the gun. Quick Murrah is a fighter but he can never be a gentleman, and I have forbidden him to speak to my daughter."

He poured out another drink and in the silence that followed Gun-smoke felt a slow flush mounting his cheeks. In the room beyond he heard Johnsie speak to her mother —then the phials of his wrath bubbled over.

"I'll tell you, Colonel," he spoke up quietly, "I applaud your sentiments about Quick Murrah, and all other cow-thieves, but if you're reaching over his shoulder to take a whack at me you can go out and ketch up my hawse. I may be travelling under a flag, but I want to tell you right now I'm a long way from being a horse-thief."

He rose up in bed and sat facing the Colonel, who was boring him through and through with steely eyes; but before either could speak Mrs. Blood came hurrying in, with Johnsie close behind her.

"Henry," she announced, "I heah Bugle up on the peaks—he's treed a lion, sure."

"Whereabouts?" demanded Colonel Blood, kicking back his chair and rushing out the door. "Dam' those hounds!" he exclaimed after a long minute of listening, "it'll spoil them if I don't ride up theah! But I'd hate to be absent when Dandy McAllister calls, as he intimated very strongly he would."

"Perhaps he's got into some poker-game," suggested Johnsie indignantly; and like a flash Gun-smoke understood. All the dressing and preparation, the excitement and the waiting, were for McAllister, the favored suitor; and the talk about Murrah and renegades in general was aimed directly at him.

"Just a moment, Colonel," he said as Blood reached for a big hunting horn and snatched down his rifle from the hook, "when you come back I expect I'll be gone. But allow me to thank you, suh, for your kindness and hospitality—only I don't stay where I know I'm not welcome."

"Oh, now, Henry!" rebuked his wife, "why can't you remember not to harp on those old ideas before our guests? And now Mistuh Gun-smoke has drawn a wrong inference and imagines you refer to him!"

"Yes, and if you're concerned about Dandy McAllister," spoke up Johnsie, "you can leave the gentleman to me. Because I'm not accustomed to wait around all day on a man that forgets his word."

"Dam' McAllister!" burst out the Colonel, drawing a cleaning stick through his rifle, does he think we must await his beck and call? Then tell him if he comes that my hounds have treed a lion, and my daughter will not see him today! And young man, you stay right heah, wheah Mrs. Blood can look after you. If you happen to get lonely I reckon Johnsie can entertain you—I'm going up the canyon, right now!"

CHAPTER V

Like a Piano

THERE was a clatter of hoofs outside the door as Heck Blood rode up the canyon, gentle protests and the kindest of smiles from his wife; and as Gun-smoke settled back on his bed to consider, a flutter of dainty skirts—and Johnsie. In that axe-hewn log cabin, with its two meager rooms furnished with bear-hides and trophies of the chase, she appeared like a vision from another world, where women were an ornament to the home. Gun-smoke had heard her surreptitiously chopping wood and bringing water while her father continued his harangues; but now she was back in her woman's sphere and she greeted him with eager eyes.

"I'm just dying," she began, "to hear about your fight. Did you actually beat Quick Murrah and win all that money? Don't you know, I couldn't believe it. And you mustn't mind Daddy, because he's such a nice man—only he's got those old-fashioned ideas. But mother was a Culpeper, from Culpeper Co'tehouse, and she claims it's the man that counts. There are so many of these rascals running around through the country who come from the very best families that she goes back of it all to the man—don't you,

LIKE A PIANO

Mother? And to think of Dad, scolding away about these Texans, when he comes from Texas himself!"

She laughed and as Gun-smoke caught the infection of her mirth he grinned and leaned back on his couch.

"First he says Quick is no gentleman," she rattled on recklessly, the better to keep him from talking, "and then he turns around and says Dandy is no fighting-man. And then he goes on to say that all the McAllisters were fighters, as if that could ever make you a gentleman, and that Dandy is just a baby that has been spoiled by his mother and therefore a disgrace to the name. Oh, he raves about him scandalous, and says it to his face; but Dandy just laughs and goes on racing horses and sitting up all night in those poker games. But if Dandy would kill Quick Murrah he'd have to fight Ed and John, because the word has gone around that the man who downs Quick will have both his brothers on his hands. And Dandy isn't a killer—he doesn't like these brawls and fights. And besides, Quick Murrah has killed sixteen men already. He's lightning, so they say, with a gun!"

"Who—him?" echoed Gun-smoke. "I thought he was just a cow-thief. By grab, I shore took a chance!"

"You shore did!" mimicked Johnsie, "and then you took a bigger one when you rode up on me after dark. I can't understand where that bullet of mine went to, because I aimed right at your heart."

"Sure enough?" he mocked. "Well, now, maybe that explains something—my heart ain't acted right since. Every time I see you coming——"

GUN-SMOKE

"Now you hush up!" she reproached, "or I'll go and call Mother." But Gun-smoke could see she was pleased.

"So I'd better apologize," he went on brazenly, "for those remarks I passed about your marksmanship."

"It seems to me," she observed, with a toss of her head, "that for a man under a flag—with two names like a piano—you're coming along awful fast. It generally takes these cowboys two days, at the least, before they lay their hearts at my feet. I only wish Dandy McAllister was listening here now—I don't care, he said he would come!"

"And didn't do it?" exclaimed Gun-smoke incredulously. "I declare, I believe your old man is right—there's something the matter with that boy!"

"The matter with him," asserted Johnsie with conviction, "is that he never did anything hard in his life. It's a long ride up here, and he's just too lazy to come."

"I'd quit him," rallied Gun-smoke, "and pick a man as was a man—some feller with two names, like a piano."

"You look out!" warned Johnsie, who was enjoying herself immensely, "I know just from looking at you that you're one of these ladies' men, but I'm liable to take you seriously. So don't you say anything you're not prepared to live up to—it gets awful lonely up this canyon."

"Oh, my Lord, I reckon that's right!" cried Gun-smoke in mock dismay; and then they both laughed at once.

"What are you children chattering about?" enquired Mrs. Blood from the kitchen, and Johnsie became instantly subdued.

"I was just telling him, Mother," she said, "about how lonely it gets here. He's sure welcome to stay, isn't he, dear?"

LIKE A PIANO

"Yes, indeed!" beamed Mrs. Blood, coming to stand in the doorway. "I only hope he won't find our little house too poor and miserable—we're hoping to furnish it, soon."

"As soon as the railroad comes, and we're rich," explained Johnsie. "But I must run now and help with the dinner."

She jumped up and fled and Gun-smoke settled back with a smile of unalloyed joy. Here was a girl after his own heart —brave and beautiful and full of life—and she was lonely for someone to talk to. Here was a queen, a Cinderella, hidden away in this rocky canyon, where Dandy McAllister was too lazy to ride. But he, Gun-smoke, had come up charging and, all joking aside, the fair Johnsie had smitten him to the heart. Only of course she was promised to McAllister. He sighed and felt his leg, which was beginning to throb again, then counted over the money he had won. With a roll like that, and what he could win racing Watch-eye, a man could settle down. But he sighed again for, much as he loved Johnsie, he loved his freedom more. And when Dandy came up for his belated visit all this foolishness would be forgotten.

He slept on the floor that night, on a couch made of buffalo-robes and bearskins piled up high; but while the Colonel told long stories beside the doorway in the morning Gun-smoke's eyes followed the girl of his dreams. He was there, and he could not help watching her, but deep down in his heart he knew he would ride away. The road to the west was calling, the road towards the setting sun, and Watch-eye came often to the door. Yet as he watched her something told him to stay.

Johnsie had dressed for the third time to receive Dandy

GUN-SMOKE

McAllister but as the day wore on and her father and mother rode away she sat down by Gun-smoke's couch.

"Oh, dear," she sighed, "I wish he'd come and have it over with, so I could go out and work in my garden. Have *you* got a girl, back there somewhere in Texas? I declare, men are all the same!"

"Sure are!" agreed Gun-smoke. "And women, too. Certainly keeps me on the move to keep some girl from roping me and putting me to work for life."

"And to think!" exclaimed Johnsie, "that I shot at you and missed you! Do you think you're as charming as all that?"

"I know it!" boasted Gun-smoke. "And now lookee here, Johnsie, don't you cry your pretty eyes out over Dandy. Because after I've had my fling and seen the great world I'm liable to come back this way."

She gazed at him inscrutably and a slow blush mounted her cheeks as her line of badinage ceased.

"I don't care," she pouted rebelliously, "he feels so darned sure of me! You may find me waiting at the gate. But Dad just insists that Gun-smoke isn't your name and—well, what do you want *me* to think?"

"Suit yourself," observed Gun-smoke with a shrug of the shoulder. "I can see he's got me down in his black books. But I'm playing a lone hand and not tipping it to no one, so the cards will have to lie as they fall."

"What are you talking about?" she demanded impatiently. "You mean you don't care what I think?"

"Oh, no!" protested Gun-smoke, "but at the same time, just going through, a man has got a right to his name.

LIKE A PIANO

Suppose I'd say I'm Bill Enright, or some such phony name, would that make it any more honest?"

"No-o, not as honest," responded Johnsie pensively. "I believe you just do it for a joke."

"Yes, and to keep these Scissor-bills from getting their beak in and trying to turn me up to some sheriff. When I tell 'em my name is Gun-smoke they take the hint and close their traps—otherwise I might write it on their hide."

He made the motion of thumbing the hammer of a six-shooter and Johnsie's eyes became veiled.

"Are you such a good shot?" she asked.

"Well, no," he jested, "there's two men back in Texas that might beat me to it on the draw."

"Yes, and I'll tell you two more," she countered swiftly. "Quick Murrah and Dandy McAllister."

"Dandy McAllister!" he echoed. "I thought he was a dude, raised a pet and all that stuff!"

"He's quicker than Murrah, only he doesn't care to fight. Sometimes I almost think he's afraid."

"And then what?" enquired Gun-smoke shrewdly.

"Never mind," she said, a smouldering anger in her eyes. "I'm a fighting Blood, myself."

"I believe it," he answered soberly. "Remember when I came here and Quick Murrah said to give me up? My hand was so weak I couldn't hold a six-shooter—and then I heard you tell him to git. I reckon you saved my life, Johnsie, but the way your old man feels maybe that wouldn't be counted no great loss. But there's something else you saved, and now that your father and mother are gone I'm going to give you your share. You saved my roll, to boot."

51

GUN-SMOKE

He fetched it out of his pocket and counted the money out in two piles while she watched him with fascinated eyes, but when he picked up one and handed it over to her she smiled and shook her head.

"I can't take your money," she said.

"Aw, I'll just lose it on some horse-race down the road," he coaxed as he met her gaze; but Johnsie turned away.

"I'm obliged to you, anyway," she answered slowly. "But what would people say?"

"Take it and bury it," he urged, "there won't anybody know." But she responded with a wry, wise smile.

"These people know everything," she stated somberly. "They're watching this house, right now. But if you'd just tell me your name———"

She paused expectantly, her eyes soft and appealing, but Gun-smoke shook his head.

"Keep your money, then!" she spoke up sharply. "How do I know it isn't stolen?" And with a flash of disdain she was gone.

CHAPTER VI

THE MASTER OF BAR C

GUN-SMOKE slept under the stars that night with his saddle at the head of his bed, and as he watched the great dipper wheel solemnly on its course he wondered if Johnsie really cared. Then he dreamed and the faithful Watch-eye, standing on three legs not far away, watched over him like a dog. But as the winds of morning rose and the stars began to pale Watch-eye sighed and stirred uneasily. It was time for his master to rouse up and go, for the coyotes were beginning to yell.

Watch-eye tramped up to the bed and breathed mysteriously into his ear as he nuzzled the yellow head; then with a short, impatient snort he nudged him wide awake and looked off down the canyon. Gun-smoke rose up cautiously, his gun in his hand, and peered out into the night.

"What's the matter with you?" he muttered as nothing moved or stirred; and Watch-eye whickered coaxingly.

"You want to go?" demanded Gun-smoke and Watch-eye nodded his head as his master sat up in bed. "Want to go off and leave that gal?" enquired Gun-smoke after a silence, and once more the pinto nodded assent. "Well, you're a hell of a horse," observed Gun-smoke reproachfully and reached under the pillow for his boots. His leg was still

GUN-SMOKE

lame, but when he tried on his left boot his foot slipped into it easily.

"Leg well, eh?" he said, and Watch-eye bumped him with his head as if urging him to get up and start. Gun-smoke stamped on his other boot and stood gazing at the cabin, where Johnsie and her parents lay asleep. What would she and the Colonel say if he sneaked away like a horse-thief, after accepting their Southern hospitality? He reached down and picked up his slicker which he had thoughtfully laid by the bed, together with his coat and guns. Had he intended all the time to slip off?

"It ain't right," he said to Watch-eye. "That's no way to treat a friend. And besides, she might give me a kiss."

At these words the attentive pinto laid his head across his shoulder and touched his cheek delicately with his lips, but Gun-smoke slapped him away.

"Quit your fooling!" he chided. "Think I want *you* to kiss me? But hell, she thinks I'm a horse-thief!"

He gazed long at the cabin, then sorted out his saddle-blankets and laid them on Watch-eye's back. He put on the bridle but as he reached down for his saddle he paused and glanced up at the house. It stood set into the hillside, bleak and plain even by starlight, telling its story of failure in the broken-down fence which had once kept the stock from the door. It was nothing—just two rooms made of stakes and daubed with mud—and yet it sheltered her.

She had asked his name and he had refused even that, but surely she was entitled to her money. He shook his head dubiously, then reached into his pocket and fetched out his roll of bills.

THE MASTER OF BAR C

"There's half," he muttered, dividing it at random in the dark, and stuffed the bills down inside the pillow-slip. Then, whipping up his saddle, he flung it on Watch-eye's back and belted on his pistols to go.

"On your way!" he ordered roughly and Watch-eye stepped off, arching his neck as he fought the bit. "She'll be mad," complained Gun-smoke as he reined in near the gate, and Watch-eye reached back and bit his leg.

"W'y, you biting fool!" burst out Gun-smoke; and when he threw the spurs into him the wily pinto jumped the gate.

"Done gone!" sighed Gun-smoke as he galloped off down the trail, and the hounds woke up and bayed his farewell. "The sweetest little gal I ever knowed—but ump-umm, no wedding bells for me!"

The sun found him on the road that he had followed from Portales and before the morning was half gone he came in sight of Barcee, the old head-quarters of the Bar C outfit. But now it was a town, two settlements in one; for across the bridge from the ranch buildings a Mexican town had sprung up, populated largely by workers on the ranch. A rushing river flowed between, and on the east bank, under the cottonwoods, the old plaza lay dreaming of the past. For here in the early days Morgan McAllister had built his fort, to shelter his *vaqueros* from the Indians; and, though the master was gone, his son still lived in the ancient Casa Grande of his father.

Mexican Town was no more than a long street lined with houses, stuck together in threes and fours by the mud of the makers, then left vacant for yards and corrals. And at each end of the street—as well as in the middle—there was

GUN-SMOKE

a big sign: CANTINA—SALOON. In two languages at once it invited the thirsty to drink, and for those who could not read there was a long line of cow-ponies standing waiting outside the doors. But Gun-smoke rode through until, crossing the bridge, he reined in before the big house.

Its doors stood hospitably open, Mexican servants peeped furtively out; but house and plaza alike were deserted by horse and man and the cause was not far to seek. On the flat beyond the whole male population was gathered in a seething crowd, and at sight of contending jockeys riding up and down the track Gun-smoke spurred out to witness the start. No one turned at his approach for the two riders were approaching the mark, and at the whang of a gun they were off like a shot, with every yelling horseman in pursuit.

Gun-smoke saw the Mexican jockey start well up in front, leaning forward with his knees through a surcingle and whipping at every jump. But behind in silk riding-tights and natty English boots, an American on a deep-blood bay was following in resistless pursuit. He caught up, he passed, he went flying past the quarter-post leaving his antagonist far behind; and one glance at his handsome face and curly brown hair told Gun-smoke that here was McAllister.

After all he had heard of the McAllister failings he was surprised to see no signs of dissipation, no mark of the brute on his face. He was a boy, fresh and smiling as he rode back from his victory, and at sight of Gun-smoke on his gorgeously painted pinto he turned and bored his way through the crowd.

"Hello!" he hailed. "Glad to see another Gringo. I'm McAllister. Come on over and have a drink."

"Sure thing," agreed Gun-smoke, reaching out to grasp his hand; and McAllister glanced appraisingly at his horse.

"Run?" he enquired, with a provocative grin; but Gun-smoke shook his head.

"Give you ten yards start," bantered McAllister. "Come on—I'd just like to see him run."

"Nope," answered Gun-smoke, "he's nothing but a cow-pony. That's a Steeldust you're riding, I reckon."

"This is a Bird-Catcher," announced McAllister with a touch of pride. "He's never been beaten yet. Can't fly, you understand, but he runs down birds—I'll give you forty yards in the half."

"Nope," returned Gun-smoke, "he's out of my class. Old Watch-eye can't run, at all."

"I know better, old sport!" retorted McAllister grinning wisely. "Happened to hear about your race at Portales."

"Oh, that!" grunted Gun-smoke. "Well, it was kinder shoved off on me—didn't have much choice in the matter. But my Dad told me not to try to show you Western fellers anything, especially about horse-racing and shooting; and I've got a hole in the back of one leg to show that the old man was right."

"Heard about it," chuckled McAllister. "So they hit you in the leg, eh? Say, is it true that you won Quick Murrah's six-shooter?"

"This is it," answered Gun-smoke, giving the gun a careless slap; and the gaping crowd stared and fell silent.

"Well, the drinks are on the house," announced McAllister, and led the way to the bar.

This was built in on one side of the huge general store

where his *vaqueros* and passing travellers bought supplies and as Gun-smoke limped in on his wounded leg he felt all eyes upon him.

"*Salud!*" greeted McAllister as he raised his glass to the crowd of Mexicans who had followed him in from the track; but after the *paisanos* had passed out he turned to his compatriot and flashed his ready smile.

"Come over to the house," he invited, "and we'll open up a bottle of old cognac. Because a man that can beat Lightfoot and win Quick Murrah's gun is certainly entitled to the best."

"All right," agreed Gun-smoke; and, stepping up on his horse, he rode over to the big house where Dandy McAllister held sway.

They went in through a garden, carefully tended by a gardener who took off his hat as they passed; then they entered a great hall with fireplaces in both corners and a floor scraped and waxed for the dance.

"Had a *baile* last night," explained Dandy McAllister as he clapped his hands for the servants; and then in fluent Spanish he rattled forth orders to his retainers, who hurried off to bring cakes and wine.

"Never lived among Mexicans, eh?" he grinned. "Well, they'll work for nothing and board themselves as long as you let 'em dance. They're good cow-hands, too—my father always used them—and they're not on the prod like these Texans."

"I'm from Texas myself," observed Gun-smoke, as they sat down by the fire; but McAllister only laughed.

"Yes, but you're no Texano!" he said. "They're a breed by themselves—I know 'em."

"Like Quick Murrah?" enquired Gun-smoke grimly; and Dandy nodded his head.

"Say," he coaxed, "give me the low-down on that scrap. The word we got here was that you beat Quick in a horse-race and they tried to hold out your money. Then the Mexicans claim you hit Plunkett over the head, grabbed the stakes and jumped your horse over the gate—but you know how these *paisanos* talk."

"Yes—and at that they didn't tell half of it," grumbled Gun-smoke. "A danged horse-thief took a shot at me while I was going down the road; and then Quick and the whole outfit chased me plumb to Blood's Canyon—claimed I stole that horse I'm riding. But I told them, and I'll tell you, that Mister Watch-eye is *mine;* and the first man that goes near him will get pawed down and jumped on—he's trained that way on purpose. Seems like every place I go some whelp tries to steal him, but nobody can touch him but me."

"Well, well!" commented McAllister; and as the drinks came on he held up his glass to Gun-smoke. "Here's to you!" he toasted. "Better stay a few days—I'd like to see this trick-horse perform."

"Trick-horse—hell!" scoffed Gun-smoke. "He's human, just like we are! Understands every word I say. He can run like an antelope, jump fences like an elk and follow a trail like a blood-hound. But he's a one-man horse and the first hombre that tries to steal him will wake up in hell with his back broke."

GUN-SMOKE

Gun-smoke paused, his eyes burning as he gazed straight ahead, and Dandy McAllister smiled.

"You think a whole lot of him, eh?"

"He's my pardner," answered Gun-smoke grimly. "I've tried folks, but Watch-eye beats 'em all."

"Going south?" enquired McAllister politely. "Glad to have you stop over a few days."

"Much obliged," grunted Gun-smoke. "Can't stop. Due in Vegas a week ago."

"Too bad," murmured McAllister, "like to have you stay for company. Lots of Mexicans around, of course, and Americans going through; but I get kind of lonely, sometimes. And by the way, how'd you leave my old friend, Colonel Blood? He's the out-fightingest Texan of them all! And, oh, yes—how's the charming Miss Johnsie?"

"All right," returned Gun-smoke, answering both questions at once, and looked Dandy McAllister over appraisingly. For five days, almost a week, Johnsie Blood had watched the trail waiting expectantly for this man to call, and he had been horse-racing and dancing with the Mexicans. Yet his mind seemed free from concern over his delinquencies as if he had kept his word.

"He's a great character, the Colonel," went on McAllister reminiscently. "Every time he comes down I throw a few drinks into him and he fights the War all over again. And not only the Late Unpleasantness, but the war with Quantrell's Guerillas and the war with Old Scorp Plunkett. Say, if hating and cussing would strike a man dead Old Scorp would have perished long ago. But the Colonel is a fighter—only nester in this country that's held out against

Murrah and the Night Riders. Although I'll tell you, Old Timer, they'd move him tomorrow except for one—no, two—things."

He leaned back and smiled but Gun-smoke waited, unruffled.

"In the first place," expounded McAllister, "the Colonel is too much of a gentleman to soil his hands by hard work. The result is his fences wouldn't hold back a goat and every cow that he steals gets out. Zim Plunkett is a thrifty soul—it sure hurts him to lose any stock—but he figures it's cheaper to keep Old Heck in beef than it is to hire Murrah to kill him. And that brings me to the second reason why the Colonel lives and prospers—he's the father of a mighty pretty daughter. When it comes to class, Johnsie Blood outholds them all, and Quick Murrah has kind of had his eye on her. Not that he has a ghost of a show, because Heck has warned him off; but you know—it makes a difference."

"Sure does," agreed Gun-smoke. "The neighbors would kill him if he tried any rough work with her."

"Well—yes and no," observed McAllister as he poured out another drink. "Because in the first place all the neighbors have been smoked out already—there aren't many nesters left. And in the second place Quick Murrah is a law unto himself. When he goes on a periodical there isn't a peace officer in this county that has got the nerve to arrest him. He hunts 'em down like rabbits—and when it comes to women he's stolen a couple that I know of."

"The hell you say!" ejaculated Gun-smoke and sat looking at him with widening eyes.

GUN-SMOKE

"They were Mexican girls, of course," qualified McAllister. "But all the same he rode in and took them."

"My God!" exclaimed Gun-smoke, "a man like that is dangerous. Suppose he'd ride up there some night and steal Johnsie!"

"We'd have to kill him," admitted McAllister, with a shrug; and Gun-Smoke muttered to himself.

"I suppose," he suggested, "you're all set to do something if the cards should happen to fall that way? Because it would take quite a bunch to tame those ZIP boys, especially if Murrah was drunk."

"He gets drunk, about once a month, and comes down and shoots up our Mexican town," answered McAllister, still with his smile. "So if you feel that we're negligent, or derelict in our duty, I'll just arrange to have you made town marshal."

"How do you mean?" enquired Gun-smoke at length.

"Well, to tell you the truth, our last marshal got killed. And so far there's been no great rush to fill his place."

McAllister smiled again and, pleasing as was his countenance, Gun-smoke detected a flicker of malice. But if he thought by guile to induce Gun-smoke to kill his enemies the master of Barcee was wrong.

"Heh—kill your own rattle-snakes," he grunted. "I'm just going through to Las Vegas."

CHAPTER VII

Good Shooting

"NOW don't hurry away!" pleaded Dandy McAllister as Gun-smoke rose to depart; but the man who was due in Las Vegas drew his mouth down and regarded him grimly.

"You're a hell of a sport," he sneered. "What are you— a man or a mouse? And Johnsie Blood was bragging you up to me as the best pistol-shot in the country. You don't need any help from *me!*"

"Oh, what's the use of talking!" cried McAllister plaintively. "You're trying the same tactics on me, now. We're all passing the hot potato, but when it comes right down to it there's nobody that will stand up to Murrah. Because why? He's killed sixteen white men. Mexicans and gentlemen of color not counted."

"Well, it's none of my business," grumbled Gun-smoke. "I'm just going through the country. But it looks like there'd be somebody with nerve enough to shoot him, if they had to wait until he was paralyzed drunk."

"There's the beauty of his system," elucidated McAllister. "When Quick gets too drunk Ed and John stand over him and fight the would-be-killers away. And if a man should kill Quick all he'd have to do then would be to kill Ed and John—both quick as lightning. Of course after that—provided he still lived—he could take on Zim Plunkett and his Night Riders. And they're a snaky band of citizens, believe me. If Zim puts your name in the little black book you might as well kiss her good-bye."

"Well, she's your girl, not mine," shrugged Gun-smoke; and Dandy McAllister laughed.

"My Lord!" he exclaimed, "has Johnsie hooked you, too? That makes it unanimous and the co'te will now adjourn—but don't take it too hard, old man. God made her what she is, and did a damned good job at it, but she just can't help using those eyes. Say, if it wasn't for her do you think Old Heck would be consuming my whisky and cigars? He just charges them at the store, because he knows his credit is good; but he's never paid a dollar—not yet! I figure it's worth the money, just to have Johnsie around here in this God-awful, man-killing country."

"Sure! Sure!" agreed Gun-smoke; but the hot blood had rushed to his cheeks—he was blushing, but without knowing it, for Johnsie. In an instant the mask of pretense had fallen away and revealed the Bloods as they were, proud pensioners of Dandy McAllister, whom they railed at while they ate his bread. Yet with all their feigned anger at his negligence they waited upon his coming, day by day. And not only as a favored suitor but as one who, when all was said, held their destiny in the hollow of his hand. He fed them, he clothed them—they were his.

"Well, got to be going," said Gun-smoke; but McAllister held up his hand.

GOOD SHOOTING

"Just a minute," he begged, "and the collation will be served. Be my guest at an A-1 Mexican dinner."

"By grab, yes!" responded Gun-smoke. "Came off without my breakfast." And McAllister roared with laughter.

"Well, all right," he choked, "I'm not asking any questions, but I'll bet you had a spat with Johnsie."

"Ump-um!" denied Gun-smoke, "Johnsie and I are great friends. I told her, just joking like, if you didn't come up to the mark——"

"But I have!" protested McAllister. "Bet I've proposed a hundred times. What gave you an idea like that?"

"Oh, you being so rich and all—and them living the way they do——"

"Nothing to it!" exclaimed McAllister. "You don't know Johnsie Blood. By the gods, she don't think I'm good enough!"

"The hell!" scoffed Gun-smoke. "Well, just how good are you?" And then they both laughed and sat down. But Gun-smoke's anxious heart had resumed its normal beat and suddenly the food looked good. And Dandy McAllister, too.

"Big outfit you've got here," observed Gun-smoke as they ate. "How does this country stack up for a cow range? I see you got lots of grass."

"Finest country in the world," boasted Dandy. "Good soil—these Mexicans can grow anything. All we need is that railroad and a little more good society to make it a cowman's paradise. But there's more cow-thieves and renegades to the nautical mile than any other place short of hell."

"Old Zim, eh?" grumbled Gun-smoke and McAllister nodded.

GUN-SMOKE

"But I try," he went on, "to take a far-sighted view of it. If that railroad wasn't coming, bringing the law and all the rest of it, I'd hire me about a hundred of the toughest gunmen I could find and clean up on these *hombres* over night. That's what you've got to do in a cow country. But in the first place, those same gunmen would probably turn on me and steal me blind in six months. And in the second place this isn't a cow country. These valleys are too fertile—they're sure to be farmed—and I'll wait and sell out to the farmers. So if I lose every hoof, as long as I keep alive, I figure I'll be winners yet."

"Sounds reasonable," agreed Gun-smoke. "How's the Mexicans?"

"Good cow-hands," sighed McAllister, "but they can't stand up to these Texicans. They're whipped before they begin."

"So you just figure on sucking the hind teat for a while, eh?" grinned Gun-smoke; and McAllister humped up his shoulders.

"Como no—why not?" he enquired in Spanish; and Gun-smoke shrugged in return.

It was nothing to him how this man met his problems—for him there was the open trail. The long way that led before him towards the setting sun—new vistas, new people, new wars. And yet he lingered and talked. Even when he went out to mount and go he stopped to give Watch-eye some grain, and as they waited McAllister glanced at his guns.

"Let me look at that pistol!" he spoke up impulsively. "The one you won from Quick Murrah. I know," he apolo-

GOOD SHOOTING

gized, "it's considered damned bad form to ask a man to look at his gun, but——"

"I've got two of them," observed Gun-smoke genially. "Just packing it along for instance."

McAllister balanced the six-shooter with a practiced hand, threw down with it and handed it back.

"It's a dandy," he said, "let's go out and try it—I do my shooting against that blank wall."

He pointed to the long wall of a warehouse which enclosed the north side of the plaza and Gun-smoke nodded assent. But before they went McAllister ordered the old gardener to bring out his other guns.

"How are you?" he enquired casually. "Pretty good shot?"

"Yes, pretty good," admitted Gun-smoke and McAllister's eyes snapped a challenge.

"Good enough to bet on it?" he asked, and Gun-smoke scratched his head.

"Nope," he decided, "the folks in this country don't seem to be very good losers. Do you want to try out Quick's gun?"

"Yes—sir!" answered Dandy instantly and as he took it he fingered it lovingly. Then, raising it slowly, he sighted long at the painted target and scored an absolute bull's-eye.

"My word!" he exclaimed as he passed it back, "that's the finest shooting gun I've ever seen. Go ahead and try it yourself."

Gun-smoke raised the polished weapon and glanced down the sights, and his too was a center shot.

"You bet," he agreed, "that's a right good gun. Notice these notches under the barrel?"

GUN-SMOKE

He pointed to three filings just in front of the cylinder and McAllister's face became grave.

"Three killings," he nodded. "Three white men. Quick'll be wanting that six-shooter back."

"Think so?" enquired Gun-smoke good-naturedly; and with three lightning shots he put three pips around the bull's-eye, then spun the cylinder to reload. "Well, he can't have it," he announced. "I'll just keep that gun myself. How are you on shooting tin cans?"

"Pretty good!" spoke up McAllister. "But if you think you can beat me I'll lay two hundred dollars against that gun."

"No-o," demurred Gun-smoke. "You might get sore if I'd beat you. After a man has just outrun one bunch of Winchesters he gets kind of bashful with strangers."

"We'll shoot for nothing, then," proposed Dandy eagerly. "Of course I know how you feel, but this isn't Portales, you know. You get a run for your money, every time."

"They gimme a run, all right," observed Gun-smoke grimly. "But you're on—we'll shoot for fun."

He threw a can in the air and punctured it neatly, McAllister hit his twice; then with three rattling shots Gun-smoke knocked his can on high and paused to load again.

"Let's shoot pebbles," suggested Dandy and when Gun-smoke gave him the gun he balanced it in his hand and sighed. "I don't suppose," he hinted, "you'd be willing to sell this?" But Gun-smoke shrugged his shoulders.

"You'd better let *me* keep it," he said. "Quick Murrah might take it away from you."

Dandy gazed at him a moment, then tossed up a pebble

GOOD SHOOTING

and smashed it to pieces in the air. He tossed up another and hit it twice, then a third and smashed two different fragments.

"That's shooting," admitted Gun-smoke; but when it came his turn he equalled it in every respect.

"Who of you will eat pebbles for me today?" demanded McAllister dramatically as he whirled on his deferential servants; and the old gardener stepped promptly forth. *"Muy bien,* Juan," he went on. "You go down and get six of them, no bigger than the end of my thumb."

A hush fell on the crowd, which grew bigger every minute as the *rat-tat* of pistol-practice announced a contest; and Gun-smoke saw that this pebble-eating, in some form or other, would turn itself into snap-shooting. Half-naked *muchachos* went dashing to summon their people, even the servants came running from the house; and as he waited Dandy McAllister took a pistol from his case and examined it with the greatest care. It was a gun with a long barrel and an extra-heavy frame to counteract the jump of the discharge; and on the polished ivory handle in an elaborate scroll there was engraved the letter M.

Old Juan returned smiling with a tin cup filled with pebbles and a small spoon, much flattened in the bowl; and with a quick, impatient gesture McAllister paced off twenty-five steps and stationed Juan before the wall. The crowd surged back to avoid the whiz of bullets, McAllister set his feet and stood firm; then with a slow, rhythmic movement Old Juan dipped up a pebble and started it towards his mouth. But between the cup and the lip there was the crack of a pistol-shot and the pebble went flying away.

GUN-SMOKE

"Otra vez!" ordered McAllister and without a tremor the old Mexican dipped again. The pistol barked spitefully and without joggling the spoon the second stone was struck in mid-air.

"That's a plenty, for me," observed Gun-smoke; but McAllister did not heed.

"Otra vez!" he called inexorably and the third stone was smashed to atoms.

The old Mexican shook his head as the rock-dust stung his face, but McAllister was not to be turned.

"Otra vez!" he challenged and, firm as a statue, Old Juan dipped, and dipped again. Five times he had lifted a pebble and each time it was shot away, and still his master shouted:

"Otra vez!"

The Mexican hesitated and smoothed out his beard, which had been shot full of acrid dust; then with a hand that dipped and trembled he scooped up the last pebble and moved it towards his lips. McAllister stood like adamant, as if to make him eat the stone; but as the people cried out his pistol barked again, knocking the pebble almost out of his mouth. Juan turned and bowed profoundly and as McAllister looked up Gun-smoke read the unspoken challenge in his eyes.

"Good! Good!" he applauded, "that's a brave *hombre*, that Mexican." Then as McAllister stood waiting as if expecting him to say something he glanced up at the swallows in the air.

"Ever shoot at one of them?" he enquired.

GOOD SHOOTING

"Lots of times," confessed McAllister, but I very seldom hit one—they turn and twist too much."

"Umm," observed Gun-smoke and drawing Murrah's pistol he balanced it thoughtfully in his hand. "I'll bet you," he said, "I can knock down the first swallow that flies across this plaza—this gun against your own."

"What—my target pistol?" cried McAllister. "Well, hardly!"

"All right," smiled Gun-smoke. "I was just trying to give you this one, only that wouldn't hardly be sporting. And if Quick Murrah came down here and tried to get it back you might think I'd done you dirt. So I'll just keep this little, gold-mounted watch-charm."

He patted the pistol fondly and slipped it back into his belt and suddenly McAllister's eyes gleamed covetously.

"I'll bet you," he offered, "I can kill one out of three—the first three that fly past that barn."

"Nope," returned Gun-smoke. "Because I know you can do it. I'm betting on what *I* can do."

"And do you mean," demanded McAllister, "that you can shoot down *any* swallow—the first one that crosses the square?"

"I don't say I can do it," stated Gun-smoke. "But I'm betting—this gun against yours."

"Well—try one!" challenged McAllister. "Try that one, up there!" And he pointed to a sleek martin, gliding past.

He slipped through the air as if it offered no resistance to the stroke of his winnowing wings. He swooped swiftly to catch a gnat, wheeled and darted away, turned lightly and spiralled back; and Gun-smoke watched him, smiling.

GUN-SMOKE

"*You* shoot him," he said at last; and McAllister whipped out his gun. Three times the pistol cracked and the swallow ducked at each shot, then swerved and whipped over the roof. "Nope—missed him," shrugged Gun-smoke. "Too far."

"Well, *you* shoot one!" cried McAllister, exasperated beyond measure. "Come on, if you're such a wonderful shot."

"Not me," returned Gun-smoke. "I'm just a common cowhand—that's sure a pretty gun you've got."

He picked up the long pistol and studied the scroll on the ivory handle—the ornate M which stood for McAllister, and Dandy's tense nerves snapped.

"You like it?" he challenged. "I'll bet it against Quick Murrah's—the first swallow that crosses the plaza!"

"A-all right," agreed Gun-smoke with a boyish grin and stood waiting, his hand at his side.

A swallow came winging past and he eyed it thoughtfully. It dipped swiftly, flying further away.

"Shoot! Shoot!" screeched McAllister. "That's our bet—you shoot that swallow or——"

Bang! spoke out the pistol and McAllister started to laugh. Then he stopped, for the swallow had dropped. Boys ran to it and brought it back, dead.

CHAPTER VIII

THE DAUGHTER OF THE STONE-EATER

"WELL, talk about your luck!" exclaimed McAllister in despair as he held up the body of the bird. "Took the top of his head off—at a hundred yards at least. I don't call that shooting, at all!"

"No?" enquired Gun-smoke. "Then what do you call it? You want to renig on that bet?"

"Hell—no!" disclaimed McAllister. "But I'll bet you a thousand dollars you can't do it over again."

"Against what?" demanded Gun-smoke. "This gun I've won?"

"Yes, that's my target-gun. I wouldn't part with it for anything. By Jupiter, I can't understand it!"

Gun-smoke gazed at his prize, then at Quick Murrah's pistol, then at his own wooden-handled six-shooter; and laughed shortly as he handed it back.

"Here—take your gun," he said. "I've got no use for it. Got more hardware than I can carry, already."

"What—really?" cried McAllister; and then he stepped back, for his hands had almost closed on the pistol.

"No!" he said. "You won it, fair and square. But I would like to buy it," he suggested.

"Buy nothing!" scoffed Gun-smoke. "It was just a friendly contest. Here, take it and I'll be on my way."

He held out the gun and McAllister laid hold of it.

"All right!" he beamed. "I'll accept it, Amigo. But if the time ever comes when I can do you a favor——"

"I'll call on you!" promised Gun-smoke, and they shook.

"You see it's this way," explained McAllister as they started towards the house. "That pistol used to belong to my father. I'd give my whole ranch before I'd part with his gun—won't you let me make you some little present?"

"Got everything I need," stated Gun-smoke, slapping his six-shooters and feeling for his makings; and McAllister gave a light-hearted laugh.

"Well, there's one thing I can do!" he said. "I'm going to show you a good time, tonight. You can forget about Vegas and the trail towards the setting sun, because you're going to stay over, as my guest. No, now I won't hear to your going, and if you do I'll be sore, so you might as well say you'll stay. We'll have music, and dancing—and some pretty *señoritas!* That ought to catch your eye!"

He slapped Gun-smoke on the back with such genuine good-humor that there was no use trying to oppose him; and besides, the long pistol-contest had taken the last of the flying hours and the sun was low in the west.

"All right," agreed Gun-smoke, "I'm just a rambling, gambling cowboy—and a man don't see a pretty Mexican girl very often."

"Oh, you don't, eh?" rallied Dandy. "Well, you wait till you see Lolita. She's the daughter of that old Mexican

THE DAUGHTER OF THE STONE-EATER

that was eating the pebbles—Juan Brabon, he's an old Indian-fighter."

"Yes, and he's one nervy *paisano*," nodded Gun-smoke. "But some day you're going to shoot his eye out."

"Not me," returned McAllister. "But even if I did it would be all right with Juan. He's one of these old-time Mexicans that thinks *El Patron* can do no wrong—worked for the family for twenty years and all that. And Lola, she thinks the same."

"The hell you say!" shrilled Gun-smoke. "You must be a winner with all the ladies. But I'm liable to cut you out."

"Cut away!" invited Dandy. "This is your night—the bridle's off. Because I think more of that pistol than I do of—well, most anything!" And he led the way into the house.

Within the thick adobe walls which had once served for a fort the light was already dim. Barred windows let in long shafts, a fire flickered fitfully, illuminating the rack of guns against the wall. Gun-smoke looked them over curiously, and every weapon that he praised McAllister instantly offered as a gift. His rash bet and the loss of his most cherished pistol had stirred him to a more than common gratitude; but Gun-smoke thought he saw something more.

Spending his life among the Mexicans he had become almost one of them—their customs and manners were his—and it is the pleasure of Spanish grandees to offer their house to every guest, although of course with no expectation of acceptance. It is merely a polite form, calling in return for a graceful declination; and in like spirit Gun-smoke declined the guns. Yet there was a long-barrelled buffalo-gun, shooting a .45-90 cartridge, which he hefted more than once. But he was travelling light, with nothing but a slicker and the two pistols that he wore in his belt, and he put it back with a sigh.

"Might borrow that sometime," he said and Dandy pressed it upon him again.

Then as evening came on the Mexican servants came in softly, bearing white linen and solid silver for the table, and in the mellow light of candles they brought in a dozen courses, each served with a different wine. There was no end to the dainties which followed the soup and fish, the salad, the beef, the beans; and as the wine loosened his tongue Dandy McAllister became more communicative, more intimate in the confidences he bestowed. But as the liqueurs were brought in and they sat chatting over their coffee, from outside the huge barred window there came the strumming of a guitar, the sweet consonance of flute, violin and harp.

"*A Sus Ojos Negros*—To Your Black Eyes!" whispered Dandy; and as the musicians without continued their serenade he lay back and smiled at the ceiling. Then, rising, he invited the invisible orchestra inside and the entertainment of the evening went on.

"Now the dancers!" demanded McAllister and, dressed in their best, bold *caballeros* and shy maidens filed in. They paced gravely through formal measures, flying swiftly into whirling waltzes which stirred even Gun-smoke's blood; but deep in his heart he had the Texan's scorn for Mexicans, a feeling which his host did not share. For Dandy more than once had bounded from his chair to join impulsively in the

THE DAUGHTER OF THE STONE-EATER

dance, and Gun-smoke noted shrewdly that it was always the same maiden that he summoned to be his partner. It was Lola, the Stone-eater's daughter, who thought the *patron* could do no wrong.

She was small and endowed with the warm, voluptuous beauty which goes so often with Latin blood; but despite the coquettish glances which she cast in his direction Gun-smoke saw he could never cut out McAllister. To please him she might smile on the yellow-haired Texano who had shot down the swallow in full flight, but her heart belonged already to the man who shot pebbles from the spoon that her father held. And not for nothing was she the Stone-eater's daughter, for she had his same resolute air. Gun-smoke smiled back boldly, the better to please his host, but he wondered how Johnsie Blood took this affair with the dark Lolita, and whether it had made her refuse him.

"And now a little pantomime!" announced McAllister to his guest. "Lolita's lover is in prison, this walled window is the door—she has come to save him from death."

He bowed to Lolita, whose eyes glowed as she met his smile, then turned down the lights for the play.

She came tripping in the doorway, bringing a platter of cooked squashes—to be given which, among the Mexicans, is the symbol of dismissal, like the old-time "giving the mitten."

"My Juan is a bold bandit," she sang, "but tomorrow at sunrise he must die."

Then at the entrance to the prison she ceased to sing his praises, for she was confronted by the stern alcalde.

"I come but to see my Juan," she sang; and then in artful

pantomime, still singing the ancient verses, she led on the imaginary alcalde until, fascinated by her wiles, he summoned the condemned lover to the door. The ardor of the alcalde increased until, yielding to his demands, she gave poor Juan the *calabasas,* at the same time slyly opening the door. Juan escapes unseen while the alcalde steals a kiss; but when her lover has safely fled the fair deceiver discovers that he has left one piece of squash in the dish. With this she brings the love-making of the alcalde to an end by dashing it into his face, and flees to join her Juan.

The pantomime was primitive, but so was Lolita, and her dark eyes were big with passion as she bowed to the Gringos' applause. And when McAllister, after dismissing the musicians, took her hand and requested her to stay her face lit up with a smile.

"This is my friend, Mr. Gun-smoke," said Dandy as he led her to Gun-smoke's chair. "I want you to sit right down here and talk your best English—he's a long way from home, and he's lonely."

He grinned and winked mischievously but Gun-smoke only smiled.

"That was sure a pretty dance you put on," he said. "But I'm jealous of this bandit, Juan."

"Nope, I'm jealous of the alcalde," put in McAllister. "He's the hombre that gets the kiss."

"No, you're wrong," answered Gun-smoke as she glanced at them shyly. "She just kissed him to save her Juan. If that sheriff that's after me should throw me into jail do you reckon she'd get me out? Or don't she like Texanos?"

"Oh, yes," she declared airily. "Some of them."

THE DAUGHTER OF THE STONE-EATER

"Do you like them with yellow hair and blue eyes?" enquired Dandy; and Lolita looked at Gun-smoke again.

"And why not?" she responded evasively. "But some Texanos are very—r-rough!"

"You mean, like Quick Murrah," nodded Gun-smoke; and suddenly Lolita went white.

"She's had a little trouble with Quick," spoke up Dandy apologetically. "He gets pretty rank when he's drunk. I expect if you'd stay over and run him out of town she'd give you a kiss, and a good one."

He grinned at her teasingly but Lolita did not smile.

"Yes," she stated. "I would."

"You hear that?" laughed Dandy. "There's your chance now, Gun-smoke—you spoke about cutting out my girl. I'll just make you town marshal and next time he comes down——"

"Nope—she's your girl," answered Gun-smoke bluffly; and McAllister gazed down at her admiringly.

"That's right," he said. "Prettiest girl in the whole country. Isn't that right now, Mister—er—Gun-smoke?"

"Prettiest girl but one," stated Gun-smoke judicially as she waited, half-smiling, for his answer. "But I saw another one, up a canyon back here——"

He paused abruptly for her eyes had suddenly changed and Dandy was flagging him to stop.

"Ha!" she exclaimed, rising up from her chair and glaring from him to McAllister. "You mean that—Johnsie Blood?"

She spat out the name so vindictively that Gun-smoke no longer had his doubts. She knew Johnsie, and Johnsie knew her, but it was time to cover his hand.

"Hell, no!" he laughed. "What gave you that idea? You think she's prettier than you are?"

"That's what Dandy says—sometimes," she answered reproachfully, and McAllister leapt up like a shot.

"Hey!" he yelled, "who started this, anyway? Come on, Lola—dance *La Botella!*"

He snatched off his coat, turning it inside out to give him a vagabond air; then, turning his trousers pockets inside out, he reached over and grabbed up a bottle.

"*La Botella!*" he cried again, thrusting it into his hip pocket and striking a rakish pose; and Lola's anger melted away like summer's snow.

"*Andele!*" she answered, snatching up another bottle, and began the first couplet of the song.

> "*Andele, compadre, baila La Botella*
> *Y si no lo bailas, yo te doy con ella!*
> Come on, compadre, dance the Bottle Dance.
> And if you don't dance it I'll give you one with this!"

She drew back the empty bottle as if to strike him and Dandy, playing drunk, responded happily.

> "*'Qui estar su compadre, bailando La Botella*
> *Y te vas a darle un besito, que sea.*
> Here is your compadre, dancing the Bottle Dance
> And you are going to give him a kiss, at least."

Lolita drew back with an expression of scorn and sang on, offering the bottle.

> "*Besitos no tengo, hay está la botella*
> *Tomas un traigo, contentas con ella.*
> Kisses have I none—there is the bottle.
> Take a drink from it, and be content."

THE DAUGHTER OF THE STONE-EATER

Dandy drew himself up and reached for the bottle, and as he finished he reached for her hand.

"Pues tomo un traigo, de sus manos, Bonita,
Y vayas conmigo a mi casa, Hijita!"
All right! I'll take a drink, from your hands, Bonita,
And then you will go with me to my house, Little Sister!"

He caught her in his arms in a very unbrotherly pose and Lolita yielded the kiss; but as they stood laughing and panting a harsh voice outside the window made them start and glance towards the door.

"Hey!" it called in a rasping, Texas twang, "Quick Murrah sent me down fur his gun!"

"Who the hell is that?" burst out Gun-smoke, rising up; and Lolita shrank back with a cry.

"It's one of Quick's Night Riders," whispered Dandy across the room; and Gun-smoke stepped closer to the wall.

"Hey—you hear me?" repeated the voice. "I want thet gun, right now. The one you stole, young feller!"

"You mean me?" spoke up Gun-smoke boldly. "Why don't he come down and get it?"

"Never mind," snarled the voice. "He'll be down hyer, damn quick, if you try any funny-business with *me*. So throw out thet pistol, right now!"

Gun-smoke drew out the gun and glanced back at McAllister, who motioned him to give it up; but Lolita standing behind him, shook her head. Then, touching her lips, she threw Gun-smoke a quick kiss and shook her head even more vigorously.

"What's the matter?" he enquired with a good-natured smile. "You want me to stay and fight?"

"Gawd—no!" burst out Dandy; but behind him, smiling radiantly, Lolita nodded her head.

"All right," he agreed. "Hey, you tell Quick Murrah to come down and get his gun!"

"He'll come!" yelled the raucous voice from the night. "He'll come and he'll come a-shootin'. We'll break you of suckin' aigs."

"Yes, you'll play hell!" jeered Gun-smoke; and turned to Dandy McAllister.

"All right, Pardner," he said. "You've got a new town marshal. I'll step in behind that badge—for one day."

CHAPTER IX

Behind the Badge

MEXICAN TOWN was deserted when the new marshal rode forth to take up the duties of the day. For one day—and perhaps a brief one—he was the embodiment of the law; and he set out to make the most of it. On the breast of his shirt there gleamed the ornate silver star which had been presented to his predecessor for valor, and Gun-smoke rolled in the saddle as he trotted up the street on the back of the vigilant Watch-eye.

In a scabbard beneath his knee he bore the heavy buffalo-gun which McAllister had had on his wall; and ready to his hands hung his old, wooden-handled pistol and the gun he had won from Quick Murrah. It was to win back this weapon that Murrah was coming—but Gun-smoke preferred to think of something else.

For no reason at all he had stayed over at Barcee—and Quick had demanded his gun. But how could Gun-smoke look Johnsie Blood in the eye if he weakened and gave it up? What else was there for a high-spirited young Texan but to wait and let him claim his revenge? For the gun was undoubtedly Gun-smoke's, won fair and square in a horse-race; and if McAllister and the Mexicans chose to bow down

GUN-SMOKE

before this bad man, that was no reason why a stranger should quit.

"Watch-eye," spoke up Gun-smoke as they ambled up the street and looked out over the long, empty road, "these folks will date time from this day. Either we go down shooting or we put the fear into the hearts of Quick Murrah and his gang. Are you afraid, Old Socks? What say?"

Watch-eye shook his head vigorously and Gun-smoke chuckled as he turned and rode back through town. From behind every barred window and from the depths of darkened doorways the Mexicans stared out like caged animals. They were afraid—afraid of the Texans, afraid of him— and he went into a saloon for a drink. Seeing them hiding almost made him afraid. But as he rode back to the bridge that separated the two towns he met Juan Brabon and Lolita.

"Kai!" he greeted as old Juan took off his hat. "How's the stone-eating business this morning?"

"He don' spik English," responded Lolita, smiling admiringly, "but the stone-eating business is good."

"Fine! Fine!" he grinned. "Did you come out to see the shooting, when I tame down these ba-ad Texanos?"

"I hope you keel that Quick!" she answered grimly.

"Sure! Sure!" he laughed. "Anything to please the ladies. Got to kill him to git that kiss?"

"No, you ron him out of town," answered Lolita, her eyes burning. "I don care — you ron him out of town."

"All right," he agreed, "I'll make him hard to ketch. What's the old man trying to say?"

"He says," she interrupted, "you look out for those Texanos. Maybeso they shoot you from behind."

"Ask him how he'd take 'em on," he suggested.

"He says," she replied, "he will go ahead and watch. And when he sees them coming, he will yell. Then, you can come and fight them, maybe."

"*Muy bien*," nodded Gun-smoke and as the Stone-eater hurried away he dismounted and sat down by the bridge.

"How do you mean—maybe?" he asked at last as Lolita lingered near; but she was staring up the road.

"Maybe they *all* will come!" she hinted.

"Say, you'd better go home," he decided, "I need all the nerve I've got. You go on back and hold hands with Dandy—I don't want to have you around."

"You think I'm afraid?" she asked.

"W'y sure!" he laughed. "The whole danged town is afraid. Never seen such a low-spirited crowd. What has Quick Murrah ever done to you?"

"He steals women," she answered vindictively; and Gun-smoke nodded wisely.

"I—I see," he said. "He tried to steal *you*. He's a bad one with women, eh?"

"I don' like him," she spat and after a glance at her sullen face Gun-smoke shrugged and looked up the road. There was a dust coming, far to the north.

"Well, you go on back," he directed, "and I'll take care of Mr. Murrah. I reckon that's him, coming."

She gazed down the street and out on the prairie beyond, and as three horsemen appeared over a swell of ground she started up to stare.

GUN-SMOKE

"Those others are his brothers," she stated. "See—there is my papá, he is watching."

Old Juan had taken his place in the middle of the street and Gun-smoke rose and tightened his cinch. Then he took down the heavy buffalo-gun and led Watch-eye out of sight behind the approach to the bridge. When he came back she was watching him intently.

"Roll your hoop, now," he said bluffly, "this is no place for little girls. And Lolita, I was just fooling about that kiss."

"How you mean?" she asked at last.

"Never mind," he answered. "You go back to the house. And don't you come out when I shoot."

He stretched out behind a timber and laid his cartridges in front of him, but Lolita did not go.

"Doggone it," he complained as he looked up and saw her, "I thought I told you to git."

"I am waiting for my papá," she responded tremulously. "But I sure hope you don' get killed."

"Same to you," he grunted. "By grab, they're sure coming!" And as the three horsemen galloped up a shrill yell rent the air and the Stone-eater waved his hat. Then with a rapid popping of pistols the riders dashed into town and reined in before the Big Cantina. In the clear morning light Gun-smoke could see their dark, gaunt faces as they searched the empty street for possible enemies—it was Quick Murrah and his brothers, come to get back his pistol, perhaps to snuff out a life. Gun-smoke glanced down the sights of the close-shooting buffalo-gun, but something stayed his hand.

They had come to kill him—he was justified in shooting

them—but he waited, and suddenly they whirled. Three hands shot into the air, three pistols spit smoke together; then with a wild Texas yell they charged through the swinging doors and Gun-smoke leapt to his feet. The time had come to strike. As well as he knew anything he knew what they were doing now—they were lined up, horse and man, for the drinks.

With a bound he ran down the bank to where Watch-eye stood waiting, thrusting the gun back into its scabbard as he mounted; then in a swift, reckless gallop he went hammering up the street and the village dogs fled yelping before him. At the door of the saloon he dropped off on his good leg and his pistols gleamed as he drew. The next moment he bulged through the door, ducked quickly to the left, and thrust them both out at once.

At the bar, with glasses poised, the three Texans sat their horses, looking back over their shoulders in surprise. They had been drinking from the stirrup, after the border cowboy fashion, but Gun-smoke had them covered with his guns.

"Hands up, you cowardly whelps!" he commanded; and they sat frozen, too startled to obey.

"Here's my badge," went on Gun-smoke. "And the first man that makes a break, I'll kill him. Glad to do it—just waiting for a chance."

Ed Murrah put up his hands, John the younger brother followed; then Quick, though he muttered an oath.

"Now git," ordered Gun-smoke peremptorily. "Out of town—and don't you come back."

He followed them through the doors and as they lined

up in the street he looked them over appraisingly. Quick Murrah had gone pale beneath the dusky tan of his Indian skin but death was lurking in his eyes. The others were afraid—they were cowed.

"Well, reach for it," taunted Gun-smoke as Quick's hand began to twitch. "Go ahead, if you're so quick on the draw. I'll just put these guns up and give you a better break." And he thrust them back into his belt.

Murrah gazed at him, keen and watchful, his little eyes moving restlessly; but he did not go for his guns.

"I was figuring," observed Gun-smoke, "on doing this country a favor by wiping you boys off the map. And now I've got you where I want you it would be a big mistake to let any one of you go. But I'm not a killer—not yet."

He paused and surveyed them quietly, and John pushed his hands up higher, but Gun-smoke shook his head.

"Nope," he said, "the wolf was plumb left out of me, but don't gamble on my good-nature too far. Now you ride out of town and don't you look back—I'm not taking any chances, at all."

He jerked his head up the road and very gently they swayed their bodies, turning their cow-ponies away from his guns. Then, still holding up their hands, they rode out of town while the Mexicans stared in silence from their doorways. Gun-smoke reached up quietly and plucked the rifle from its scabbard, the better to keep them in range, but not even Quick looked back. For a hundred yards, for four hundred yards they trotted away, their hands extended; and the Mexicans crowded into the street. Then with a shrill, defiant yell Quick snatched out his pistol and fired it into the air as he turned.

But Gun-smoke had been waiting, his buffalo-gun poised, and as Quick Murrah whirled to shoot the heavy rifle leapt up and its roar woke the echoes of the town. The left side of Murrah's coat was ripped off and hurled away. His hand jumped and he let his pistol fall. But the bullet had missed his heart, grazing the ribs as it passed, even burning the inside of his arm. Gun-smoke jacked up another cartridge, then turned to the Stone-eater, who had suddenly stepped out of a doorway.

"How's that for close shooting?" he enquired.

Old Juan racked his brains for enough English to express his thoughts; then, doffing his hat, he picked up a small pebble and held it aloft between two fingers.

"You shoot!" he invited and as the Mexicans observed his pantomime, they burst into roars of laughter. It was a very small pebble, no bigger than a buckshot, and Gun-smoke bowed in acknowledgment of the compliment.

Down the road in a cloud of dust the three Texans were in full flight, the marshal's duties were done; but as he limped over to Watch-eye who was snorting to go Lolita came running up the street. Her face was alight, there was a world of gladness in her smile, and as he stood there dumfounded she threw her arms about his neck and kissed him again and again.

"That's enough now," he laughed as he pulled her hands away. "I was just fooling about that kiss."

But as he met her eyes his face became suddenly grave. For Lolita was not fooling.

GUN-SMOKE

"Hell!" he muttered as he swung up on his horse. "I've been and gone and done it again. All quiet in town, eh? Give that to McAllister!" And he threw his marshal's badge into the street. Then with a bow to the startled Mexicans and a last glance at Lolita he galloped away to the south.

CHAPTER X

THE WHITE WOLF

"DOGGONE it," grumbled Gun-smoke as he looked back at Barcee, "there's another burg I can't go back to. What's the matter with these womenfolks, anyway?"

Watch-eye swivelled one ear back to catch the words of his master, then pointed them both to the front.

"Who'd a thought," complained Gun-smoke, "that a Mexican girl like her would kiss a cussed Texano! And McAllister's girl, at that! Well, down the road, Watch-eye—down the road towards the setting sun! Danged lucky to git off alive."

Watch-eye arched his proud neck and his glassy eyes gleamed; then, making a baulk to bite his leg, he settled down to his steady road-gait and Gun-smoke heaved a sigh. Some strange fatality seemed to dog his steps, making fighting men his enemies and women his friends—but before him lay the open trail. He was free, all the world was before him—new faces, new adventures, new friends. And all his enemies were left behind—all his quarrels and mistakes and budding love-affairs. It was better so, after all.

Yet as he rode on he pondered on the Stone-eater's daughter and why she should give him a kiss. Only the

GUN-SMOKE

evening before he had read her secret in her eyes—she was in love with McAllister, her *patron*. It was to tease him that, in jest, Gun-smoke had made the pretended bargain, to drive Murrah out of town for a kiss. But his honor as a fighting man had made him meet the Texans, and refuse to give up his gun. If it was kisses that he sought he had no need to roam so far, but women could never understand.

He sighed and threw the spurs into the dawdling Watch-eye, who was making furtive grabs at bunches of grass, but as the miles fell behind him his mind went back up the trail to the cabin hidden away in the hills. When Johnsie heard of his close shooting and his encounter with Quick Murrah perhaps she would forget how he had dropped out of sight, without a word, like a thief in the night. He had had no thought, with her, of asking for a kiss; yet he wondered, since women are human, what her answer might have been if he had said what was in his heart.

It was just for that reason, that women are so human, that he had left without saying good-bye; for though she took him for a horse-thief Johnsie was lonely up her canyon, and he might say something he would regret. And she, being lonely and at outs with Dandy, might forget and answer: "Yes." And then what? Ah, there was the rub, for Gun-smoke did not want to settle down. Not even for Johnsie would he live in one walled canyon or in one spot on the boundless plains. There was that in his blood which urged him on and on, whether they treated him well or ill. He was a rambling, gambling cowboy, and the open trail was his home.

The Las Vegas trail skirted the base of the towering

THE WHITE WOLF

Rockies, leading up over long ridges and down across wide swales which opened up onto the plains. Cattle grazed along the hillsides or scattered out in tiny dots over the sea of grass below and as he dismounted to rest his leg, which was beginning to throb and ache, Gun-smoke saw a lone horseman, far behind. He was following him down the trail. Gun-smoke watched him idly as Watch-eye cropped the grama-grass, and at the next little rise there were two. They rode on down the trail, and behind them came two more, riding fast to catch up with the first.

"What the devil!" grumbled Gun-smoke and, remembering certain hard faces, he mounted and spurred on to the south. But now he thought no more of the fair ones left behind—in their place there flashed up visions of Zim Plunkett and Cutthroat Charley, of Quick Murrah and his galloping horsemen. He had beaten them and escaped; but were they following now to kill him, to ride him down on the plains? He halted behind the summit of a ridge and crept back cautiously to look.

Where two men had ridden before, with two following behind, there were four now, with two more behind. Nor did they turn out to ride through the cattle which grazed on both sides of the road. These were men with some purpose beside that of reading brands—they were following on his trail. Gun-smoke glanced up at the sun, which was swinging down towards the west, and rode steadily on as before; but behind the next ridge he stopped and looked back—there were more riders now, there were ten!

"Old Scorp!" he pronounced, limping back to mount and ride. He had not yet escaped the Night Riders. Yet if he

GUN-SMOKE

fled they would follow and he kept his even gait until dusk cast a haze over the hills. Then he swung out over the rocks, to leave no tracks for their trailers, and rode for the open plains. He hit a high lope as he broke out of the foothills; and as the night came on he circled and rode due north, in the direction from which he had come. So foxes, when hard pressed, doubled back on the hounds, and he laughed as he rode through the dark.

On the trail far behind him a signal-fire blazed up, winking the message of his escape; and soon, on the ridge just south of Barcee, an answering fire blinked and beckoned. The hunt was on, with many riders scouring the prairie or riding pell-mell towards Las Vegas; but beneath the quiet stars Gun-smoke rode back softly, keeping well down in the shelter of the draws. Watch-eye fell into a cow-trail that led on across a stream, the lights of Barcee twinkled behind; and at last, far out on the grassy plain, Gun-smoke reined in and stepped wearily down.

For a long time he stood listening to the sounds of the summer night, the lonely hooting of ground-owls, the roar of swooping night-hawks, the far-away howl of a wolf; and as he listened the vigilant Watch-eye raised his nose to the wind and sniffed it with reassuring snorts.

"All right, eh?" muttered Gun-smoke, "my leg hurts like hell." And stripping off his saddle and bridle he turned his trusty mount loose. Not even a hackamore dragged after Watch-eye as he walked—he was free as the prairie wind— but as Gun-smoke made his bed in a buffalo-wallow he came and stood above him. Gun-smoke rubbed his soft nose, brushing the hair out of his eyes and caressing his sensitive ears;

THE WHITE WOLF

then he pulled off his boots and settled back with a sigh while Watch-eye chomped away, on guard.

Midnight came, and a taint on the wind wakened Watch-eye as he stood drowsing by the wallow. He raised his head and listened, softly inhaling the burdened air and blowing it out with low snorts. Gun-smoke stirred and snuggled closer beneath his sweaty saddle-blanket, and Watch-eye breathed warningly in his ear.

"What's the matter?" grumbled Gun-smoke as Watch-eye gave a huge snort and jumped back as if to run; and peering over the edge of his hiding-place he stared out into the night. A ghostly form, white and mowing, appeared in the darkness, and Gun-smoke settled back with a grunt. It was a wolf, probably attracted by the tallow on his throw-rope or creeping up to steal his boots. He dropped back, but as he slept Watch-eye jumped even more violently and whistled forth a challenge of fear.

The wolf was closer now and Gun-smoke reached for his gun, but to shoot would summon his enemies—he would have to saddle and ride. He picked up a clod of dirt from the side of the hole and hurled it with a curse at the ghost, then muttered as the brute made off. Sleep was heavy upon him now and when Watch-eye, snorting anxiously, reached down and nudged him awake he slapped him away and slumbered on. But when with a fierce whistle he snorted danger into his ear Gun-smoke reached for his pistol and looked out.

Almost at the brink of his hiding-place the grey wolf stood swaying its head. Gun-smoke stared at it intently, for its actions were suspicious and Watch-eye was exploding with angry snorts. Whether he fired or not there was no more sleep for Gun-smoke with this creature prowling about and at last with a vengeful curse he thrust out his pistol and shot.

"Take that, you danged whelp," he muttered as the wolf fell kicking and lay still; then, heaving up impatiently, he pulled on his tight boots and stumbled out of the hole.

"Come up here, you crazy fool!" he burst out petulantly as Watch-eye stood snorting at the wolf; but for once the pinto refused to obey. Every breath was an explosion, and Gun-smoke laid down his bridle while his hand crept back to his gun. Then swiftly he glided over and touched the muzzle to the wolf, which lay dead in a pool of blood. Something dark appeared behind it, something white reached out in front. He jumped—it was a human hand.

"Gawd A'mighty!" breathed Gun-smoke as he stood staring at the body; and in the grass before the outstretched hand he beheld a huge pistol, cocked. The wolf-skin had cloaked a man—a murderer, creeping up to kill him—but his first shot had laid him low. Gun-smoke snatched away the hide and leaned down to scan the face. He had guessed right—it was Cutthroat Charley.

In some mysterious way he had traced Gun-smoke to his hiding-place, but his wolf-skin had not deceived the faithful Watch-eye and his criminal career had been brought to a close. Gun-smoke stood over the horse-thief, the first man he had ever killed, gazing with awe at the outstretched hand which had been thrust out to shoot him, noting the white line across his throat. There the hangman's noose had cut before they lowered him to the ground and ordered him to steal no more; but Gun-smoke's beautiful pinto had tempted him beyond his strength, and now he had paid the price.

Gun-smoke reached for his saddle, to mount and ride away from this grisly, sinister form; but as he was tightening up the latigos Watch-eye snorted and wheeled and a voice came out of the night.

"Did you kill the son-of-a-goat, Charley?"

It was like the slap of an unseen hand and Gun-smoke turned with an oath.

"No," he growled and crouched closer to the ground to sky-line this gloating assassin. There was a thud of horses' feet, an impatient jerk, and looming against the sky Gun-smoke saw a tall rider, dragging Charley's reluctant mount behind.

"Did you kill the danged whelp?" he cried out exultantly and Gun-smoke felt the strong lust to slay.

"No!" he snarled, "but I will!" And his gun leapt up of itself. There was a flare of light, the deep-mouthed *bang* of the six-shooter, and the tall man went over backwards. But Gun-smoke did not wait to investigate. As the two horses broke and fled he swung up on Watch-eye and galloped off into the night.

His blood was pounding now, he felt a fever in his brain and Watch-eye spurned the ground as he ran; but in front of them to the south two shots stabbed the darkness and Gun-smoke pulled up short. Two shots from behind, where Cutthroat Charley had met his death, spat out their sinister answer; then two more, far off to the east. Gun-smoke reined towards the west and rode at a gallop, dimly conscious of an outdistanced pursuit. But day would soon

GUN-SMOKE

come, and with the Night Riders on his trail he felt the hunted man's instinct to hide.

The huge bulk of the mountains rose before him as he rode and he turned up a wide, grassy swale; but when he slowed to a walk he heard drumming hoof-beats behind him, then two shots and a long, shrill whistle. He was just starting up the wash when two more shots flashed in front of him—he was surrounded, he was caught in a great circle.

"To hell with 'em!" cursed Gun-smoke recklessly and charged forward to break through the line. What was one man to him—he had shot two already! And if he tarried the big circle would close in and net him—he swung low and rode for the hills. It was dark, but in the gloom a broad line appeared before him, a white trail leading to the south. Then Watch-eye shied violently and as Gun-smoke hooked the horn he heard the *bang* of a pistol-shot.

Watch-eye had turned and swung north at a gallop, taking the curves at lightning speed. Gun-smoke felt a hard blow, as if something had struck his crazy-bone; then a six-shooter spat out at him, close behind. He turned in the saddle and emptied his own in five swift shots, straight into the answering blaze. They whirled around a point, the horseman close upon him and their pistols exchanged fire again. But at the next dip into a canyon the man was not there—only his mount, running wild down the trail. Gun-smoke swerved to the left and hid up a little wash as the riderless horse clattered by. But on its heels came another horse, and another behind that, and he reined behind a bush and sat still.

Up the trail at a furious gallop the pursuing horsemen

THE WHITE WOLF

spurred on and on and as their clatter died out Gun-smoke headed for the hills, for suddenly he felt sick and weak. Then the black night went blacker, and he pitched off his horse into the sand. He roused from his faint to find Watch-eye snuffing him curiously and his shirt-sleeve wet with blood, and with a curse he stumbled to his feet. He had been hit, he was wounded again, and if the Night Riders found him there would be no escape this time from death.

Groaning and groping for the horn he hauled himself laboriously into the saddle. With numbing fingers he loosened his rope. Then, wrapping it around him, he made the ends fast and touched the anxious Watch-eye with his spurs. The night closed in again like the shadow of approaching death and Watch-eye plodded away into the darkness.

CHAPTER XI

Two Lumps of Sugar

GUN-SMOKE had ridden fast and far before the bullet of the Night Rider had caused him to seek the hills but when he roused up, still tied to the saddle, and gazed about with blood-shot eyes he wondered which was the dream. Had he dreamed that Cutthroat Charley had crept up to his bed disguised as a prairie-wolf? Had he dreamed that in hot anger he had shot another rider and engaged in battle with a third? Or was he dreaming now that he was back in Blood's Canyon and Watch-eye was nosing at the bars?

The pinto set his strong teeth into the topmost pole and rattled it back and forth, then with a quick flip to the right he jerked it loose and it fell with a clatter to the ground. Gun-smoke glanced at the rope that bound him to the saddle-horn, at the blood which had sopped his shirt. He was hurt, and back at Blood's Canyon; but his fight had taken place on the plains. Watch-eye pushed out another bar and stepped gingerly over the rest as he plodded on up towards the house. Good old Watch-eye—he had brought him home!

At the clatter of falling bars a hound pealed out his challenge, others rushed from their bed under the house; and as Gun-smoke's brain cleared he saw the door jerked violently open and the Colonel stepped forth with a gun.

"Heah!" he called, "what the devil are you doing? Now you git, and nevah come back! You're no gentleman, suh—sneaking off in the night like the low-down hawse-thief you are!"

"Wha's that?" enquired Gun-smoke groggily. "Say, gimme a drink, will you, Colonel?"

"A drink!" repeated the Colonel with biting scorn, "you've had too many already. And after a night in the barroom—and a fight, too, if I'm a judge—you come back to the man you've insulted."

"Gimme a drink!" repeated Gun-smoke insistently; and from the open door behind Johnsie Blood came bounding out.

"Oh, he's hurt!" she cried reproachfully. "Why, I do believe he's shot." She ran closer and stared up through the greying dawn, and then she gave a shriek.

"He's killed!" she screamed. "He's tied into the saddle and the blood has run down everywhere!"

"Got shot—by the Night Riders," responded Gun-smoke thickly. "Up here," and he touched his shoulder.

"Oh, mercy!" exclaimed Mrs. Blood, running out to join her husband who was lifting Gun-smoke out of his saddle, "I knew he'd never escape alive! They're determined to kill us all, it's just a matter of time! Oh, Henry, let's give up—let's go!"

"Stop your chatter!" scolded the Colonel, "Mistuh Gun-smoke is badly hurt. And if the Night Riders did this he's

GUN-SMOKE

welcome to my home, no matter how many hawses he's stole."

"He never stole any horses," wailed Johnsie despairingly. "Oh, where did they shoot him now?"

"Through the back!" cursed the Colonel, "the way they always shoot, the cowardly passel of assassins. He's shot high, through the shoulder—we'll put him in our bed!" And they bore Gun-smoke into the house.

He awoke to find the Colonel standing over him curiously with Mrs. Blood and Johnsie behind.

"Don't move, now," he said. "You've been shot through the shoulder and hurt your leg, to boot. Are the Night Riders on your trail?"

Gun-smoke rolled his eyes as he tried to collect his thoughts—and then he remembered Watch-eye.

"Say, where's my horse?" he demanded.

"He's heah," answered Colonel Blood grimly. "Do you want him inside, as usual?"

"I'll take care of him," volunteered Johnsie eagerly; but Gun-smoke shook his head.

"You look out," he warned, "he's liable to paw you down. Open the door while I talk to him first."

He thrust a finger into his mouth and gave a shrill whistle and Watch-eye came trotting to the house.

"I'll speak to him," he said, "and tell him not to bite you." But Johnsie only laughed.

"Aw, Watch-eye won't hurt me," she scoffed and strode out the open door.

"You Watch-eve!" called Gun-smoke, "don't you kick her or I'll kill you!"

TWO LUMPS OF SUGAR

"Now you hush up!" she called back. "He's perfectly gentle, and I know it. Whoa, boy!" And she loosened the cinch. Then while Gun-smoke shouted orders she stripped off saddle and bridle and hit Watch-eye with the reins over the rump.

"Go on, horse," she said. "And don't mind him—he's crazy!" But Gun-smoke did not answer her smile.

"Don't you spoil my horse," he croaked. "Don't you feed him now, while I'm sick. He's a one-man horse, understand?"

"All right," she answered lightly and at a glance from her father she turned and went away.

"Now, young man," began the Colonel, "if you can get your mind off that hawse for a minute, I'd like to have a little information. Wheah were you when you got this wound?"

"Down on the road," replied Gun-smoke; and as briefly as possible he outlined his running fight.

"Good! Good!" pronounced the Colonel. "So you killed Cutthroat Charley! He was the worst villain unhung in these parts—except Zim Plunkett and Quick Murrah, of co'se. Now what was all this fighting down in Barcee yesterday? I heard you had a run-in with Quick!"

"Yes, and a run-out!" boasted Gun-smoke. "I ran him plumb out of town. They made me town marshal—for one day."

"Didn't he fight?" enquired Colonel Blood dubiously.

"Hell—no!" scoffed Gun-smoke. "He was afraid to. His two brothers were there, too, and I run them out with him. You should of heard them Mexicans laugh!"

GUN-SMOKE

"Now, don't get excited," soothed the Colonel, feeling his brow. "You've got a big hole in your back—just grazed your collar-bone, passing out. But I can hardly believe that last."

"You can't hardly believe anything!" retorted Gun-smoke heatedly. "But I did it, all the same. You just ask Dandy McAllister—he knows."

"Ah, was Dandy theah?" asked the Colonel with sudden interest. "So that was why Quick left town!"

"*No!*" shrilled Gun-smoke. "He was back in his house. But his Mexican, that Stone-eater, was there."

"What? Dandy not present?" exclaimed Colonel Blood; and he turned to glance at his wife.

"Well, it wasn't his funeral!" defended Gun-smoke. "I didn't need any help, with those yaps."

"Well, well!" frowned the Colonel, "this is very unusual. I understand you were Dandy's guest."

"What difference does that make?" demanded Gun-smoke and Colonel Blood threw his head up arrogantly.

"It makes this difference, suh," he stated. "You were his guest and theahfore his friend. And it is the custom, among gentlemen——"

"Oh, now Henry!" protested Mrs. Blood anxiously, "please don't get Mistuh—er—Gun-smoke excited."

"He's all right—perfectly calm," answered the Colonel shortly. "But very well—some other time."

He strode out in a huff and Mrs. Blood bustled about, cleaning Gun-smoke up and bringing his breakfast; but it was easy to see she was worried. Her kind, motherly eyes glanced often at the door and when at last they were alone

104

TWO LUMPS OF SUGAR

she hurried in with a pillow-slip which she passed over furtively to her guest.

"I knew you'd remember it," she explained. "I suppose you came back after this."

"After what?" enquired Gun-smoke blankly.

"Why, your money!" she exclaimed. "You went off and left it. And oh, I was so worried for fear Henry might find it and not understand, you know. He might think you were trying to pay us and——"

Gun-smoke caught it like a flash—the insult to their pride which such a payment would convey—and he passed it off with a laugh.

"My Lord!" he cried, "did I go off and leave my roll? Say, that's where I put it—in that pillow-case."

He chuckled to himself as he fetched out the wadded bills and Mrs. Blood beamed triumphantly.

"I told her!" she said. "I told her you were just young and careless; and forgot, the way boys often do."

"Forgot several things," admitted Gun-smoke tucking the bills under his pillow. "But I was leaving kinder early and —well, I didn't stop to thank you for your kindness. You certainly entertained me with true Southern hospitality, and I hoped to thank you later."

"You were welcome, of co'se," she smiled, "and we were sorry to have you go, but—*Now,* you're doing the same thing right over again!"

She snatched the bills out from under his pillow and laughed as Johnsie glanced in through the doorway.

"See what this foolish boy was doing—again!" she cried. "He was putting his money inside the pillow-slip!"

"Well, you've got my clothes!" complained Gun-smoke. "Where else could I cache it, anyway?"

"I'll take care of it for you!" she offered and went out smiling happily; but Johnsie looked him straight in the eye.

"You can't fool me," she said, sitting down and surveying him accusingly. "You thought you'd play smart and leave that money, anyway—after I'd told you I couldn't receive it! And then you sneaked away, like some horse-thief!"

"Well, that's what you thought I was," defended Gun-smoke weakly; but he dared not meet her eye.

"I'd think so yet," she stated, "only you haven't got sense enough—leaving your money around in pillow-slips! Suppose some officer should come here and find all those bills? Do you think that's quite fair to your friends?"

"By grab," he grumbled, "you've got the worst case of suspiciousness that I've run across in years. Didn't I tell you I win that money on a horse-race?"

"Yes, and you told me your name was Gun-smoke!" she flared back. "And that's one thing I just know is a lie."

"Well, call me Bad Medicine, or Bill Enright or anything. As Shakespeare says—what's in a name?"

"A real name shows you're honest, and on the square!" she replied. "But whoever heard of a family named Gun-smoke?"

"This is a case," he grinned, "where, as Shakespeare says again, a man's actions speak louder than words. Ain't I lived right up to that name?"

"Oh, what do you know about Shakespeare?" she flouted. "I declare, I believe you're just bluffing. You haven't done anything but, just to act tough, you——"

TWO LUMPS OF SUGAR

"Say, kid," he nodded admiringly, "they can't fool you much, can they? You just keep right on thinking that way and it'll sure relieve my mind, because I've got to preserve my *incognito!*"

"Your which?" enquired Johnsie, and then she laughed heartily. "You've been reading some book," she said.

"Oh, well," he sighed, "I see you'll never take me seriously so I might as well get well and go. You think much reading has made me mad, eh?"

"Maybe you had a good start," she jested, "before you ever got a-hold of Shakespeare."

"Nope, it wasn't that," he confided. "I was perfectly O.K. until I rode up this canyon and seen you. Since then I haven't been right."

"I believe it," she nodded with conviction. "But at the same time," she added bitterly, "I never thought you'd ride away without even saying: Good-bye."

Her lips trembled a little now and a new soberness came over Gun-smoke as he saw the hurt look in her eyes.

"I'll tell you, Johnsie," he said, "I didn't dast to do it. Because if I had I'd——"

He paused and sighed.

"You'd what?" she prompted.

"I'd said something I might be sorry for."

"Oh, I see," she nodded. "Well, don't worry. So you didn't intend to come back at all, then?"

"Nope," he confessed. "And I can't figure out yet how I got here. I was fifty miles away when this ruckus began, and seems like they chased me a good fifty more; but when I got this hit I just tied myself in the saddle and turned

GUN-SMOKE

old Watch-eye loose. Next thing I knowed I was here."

"Well, that's too bad," she mocked. "And then the *next* thing you knowed, Johnsie Blood was back making eyes at you!"

"Hell—no!" he grinned. "I was biting my tongue to keep from saying how pretty she looked."

"Well, well," she smiled, "the boy is improving. Must have had some practice, sometime. But go right on—we make it a principle in this country never to pry into anybody's past."

"Practice—nothing!" he scoffed. "It just come to me natural, whenever I look up and see you. But your mother told me, Johnsie, not to get wrought up or excited, so I won't try to tell you the rest."

"No—don't," she said, laying a cool hand on his brow. "Just lie back and go to sleep and think how wonderful it is not to have to say anything at all. And when you wake up I'll try to think of something pleasant, instead of all the spiteful things I've said. And don't worry, Mr. Gun-smoke, about anything *you've* said, because I know you're not responsible. A man with a horse that's smarter than he is has nothing to fear from me."

She rose up and went out, and while Gun-smoke was asleep she gave Watch-eye two lumps of sugar.

CHAPTER XII

The Smartest Cowman in Texas

WHEN his fever abated Gun-smoke noted a new solicitude on the part of Johnsie and her mother; but when the Colonel did not respond to the baying of his hound pack he knew that something was wrong. Then he noticed that the women kept the outer door closed, glancing often through the loop-hole at the trail, and he guessed what was on their minds. He had come back, bringing the anger of the Night Riders upon them, and every minute they expected the attack.

"Colonel," he began, when he had him alone, "as soon as I can ride I'll be leaving here. Is Zim Plunkett after me again?"

"Yes, he is," admitted the Colonel, "and theah's no use denying it—he's watching our cabin, right now. But don't you worry, young man—you're more than welcome to stay heah, if you can put up with our humble fare."

"Colonel," protested Gun-smoke, "I feel like a dog, bringing the Night Riders on your neck again. And honestly, I didn't intend to do it. But when I got hit I just tied myself into the saddle and turned Watch-eye's head toward the hills."

"So my daughter informs me," returned Colonel Blood

GUN-SMOKE

grimly. "But as I said befoah, if you can put up with our hard fare——"

"W'y, Colonel," exclaimed Gun-smoke, "I'm living like a king. These big steaks are building me up better than anything in the world, and your wife is giving me everything!"

"Amy's a good cook," conceded the Colonel. "We don't live so bad. But these rascals in the hills are watching me so closely I can't get away to kill a deer."

"Give me beef," pronounced Gun-smoke, "and you can have all the deer-meat. But who do you reckon these hombres are that are watching the house so close?"

"Quick Murrah and his gang," answered Heck Blood ominously. "They've got you marked for death."

"Let 'em mark!" scoffed Gun-smoke, "I could've killed all three of them, only I can't shoot down a man in cold blood."

"They can—that's the difference," responded the Colonel. "And you'll never leave this canyon alive, if Quick Murrah has his way. You humiliated him and his brothers before those Barcee Mexicans and they're watching this house, day and night."

"You wait till my arm gets well," threatened Gun-smoke, "and I'll chase them like a goat. He don't look bad to me—and next time we have a run-in I'll jump him out and *make* him fight.'

"He'll fight," replied the Colonel, "have no doubts about that. He's a killer, through and through, and quick as a rattlesnake. He'll pistol you before you know it."

"Think so?" smiled Gun-smoke. "I'm kinder quick, myself. Did they tell you about me winning Dandy McAllister's six-shooter, winging swallows at ninety yards?"

"They told me," admitted the Colonel, "but a thing like that could happen only once in a lifetime. Quick Murrah has practiced the draw until the action can't be seen—it's too swift for the human eye; so my advice to you is to shoot it out in the open, with rifles. I see you've got a good one on your saddle."

"Oh, that one," nodded Gun-smoke. "Little present from Dandy—and believe me, it shoots to a hair. At four hundred yards I took Quick Murrah's shirt off, and I'll bet it broke his nerve, to boot."

"Mistuh—ah—Gun-smoke," spoke up the Colonel after a contemplative silence, "I don't know who you are, but somehow I like your style. You may be a trifle boastful, but I'll have to admit you have acquitted yourself very creditably. At the same time you've been shot twice in less than two weeks; and it's only a matter of time, if you remain in this country, until Quick and his killers will get you. I admire your courage, but my advice to you is to leave these renegades alone. Because, no matter how brave a man is, a bullet will kill him."

"There's something to that," responded Gun-smoke soberly; and the Colonel laid a hand on his arm.

"You stay heah," he said, "until you get well. And then some dark night you take your hawse and ride—and don't stop until you're clear back in Texas. That's my advice, now, as a friend."

"Well—I'll do it," decided Gun-smoke. "That is," he added quickly, "if you don't need me here. But you've taken

GUN-SMOKE

me in twice, Colonel, when those hell-hounds were after me, and I never go back on a friend. Right or wrong, I'll fight for him—and after what you folks have done——"

"No, my boy," smiled the Colonel, "I'm proud to hear you say it, but we don't need your help—not right now. Zim Plunkett has learned to let sleeping dogs lie, and I'm tired of this uphill fight. I'm whipped, only I won't admit it, so I've decided to wait for the railroad."

"Well, now, Colonel," went on Gun-smoke with a mysterious smile, "I've been studying over Zim Plunkett, and I don't know whether you're whipped or not. I believe there's a way of pulling his teeth—have you got those notes he gave you?"

"I have," responded the Colonel, "right over in that trunk, but they're not worth the paper they're written on. Because Scorp Plunkett has been outlawed in the State of Texas, and he'll never set foot across the line."

"At the same time," suggested Gun-smoke with a meaning smile, "he might be induced to do so. There are ways of doing everything and I'm willing to take a chance, if you'll give me a little help. All I want is the name of every man that's holding those notes—believe I'll go back and buy 'em up."

"They're worthless," declared the Colonel impatiently. "He'll never go back to Texas, and if he did he wouldn't pay a dollar."

"I'll tell you," spoke up Gun-smoke impulsively, "you may think I'm a horse-thief, trying to outrun the sheriff; but I've got folks, my ownself—my dad is the smartest cowman in Texas!"

THE SMARTEST COWMAN IN TEXAS

"This will be good news for Johnsie," beamed the Colonel, "because she just naturally despises a hawse-thief."

"Never mind about Johnsie," cut in Gun-smoke. "I'm telling you about my dad. He's the man to take Old Scorp and tie him up in a bow knot. He'll figure out some way of getting him over into Texas—and believe me, he'll collect on those notes. No, I know *you* couldn't do it, and neither could I; but my old man is a wolf. Never did a crooked thing in his life; but he's just naturally smart in a trade, and that's the way to git Zim Plunkett. There's no use trying to fight him. But you touch his pocket and you touch his heart; and I'll bet my father can clean him!"

"Very praiseworthy opinion," commented the Colonel dryly, "glad to heah you speak so well of your father. But you'll pardon me for doubting if he or any other man can get the better of Scorp in a trade."

"No, go ahead and doubt!" flared back Gun-smoke. "You must think I'm crazy as hell! But I'll tell you what I'll do—I'll buy those notes of yours for ten cents on the dollar, right now!"

"And then what?" queried the Colonel shrewdly.

"I'll go back to my old man," answered Gun-smoke confidently, "and he'll hang Plunkett's hide on the fence. Never mind how—he can do it. All I need right now is those notes."

"Very well, suh," spoke up the Colonel, "I'll just turn them over to you. And I'm proud indeed to know you have such a father—you can pay me the ten per cent later."

"Nope—spot cash!" returned Gun-smoke, running his hand under his pillow. "Say, gimme my clothes, will you—

Mrs. Blood done hid my roll for fear I'd lose it or something."

For a moment Heck Blood stood eyeing him sternly, for he had heard about the money in the pillow; then he restored the hidden pillow-slip and got his notes from the trunk while Gun-smoke counted his roll.

"There's some more in my clothes," he said at last. "How much do those notes of yours come to?"

"Well—twenty thousand dollars," stated the Colonel. "I sold him two thousand head at ten—but of co'se you wouldn't want them all."

"I'll go the limit," answered Gun-smoke, "as long as my money lasts. Just pass me over them pants."

He went through the various pockets, culling out more and more money until the Colonel began to stare. Then, ripping open a seam, he reached down inside the waistband and fetched out eight hundred-dollar bills.

"There you are," he said. "Two thousand dollars even, and I'll ask you to sign over those notes."

"Who to?" enquired the Colonel politely.

"Well—make it to Bill Enright," decided Gun-smoke at last and Heck Blood grunted as he passed over the notes.

"Very well," he said. "Your name means nothing to me. But to my daughter, now——"

"Never mind," spoke up Gun-smoke in a huff. "I reckon my folks are just as good as any. And if your daughter don't like my name she'll have to think up another one, or just let it go for plain Smoke."

"That's agreeable to me," responded the Colonel stiffly. "Only it's customary, among gentlemen——"

THE SMARTEST COWMAN IN TEXAS

"Colonel Blood," broke in Gun-smoke, "a man can be a gentleman with any name, or no name at all. It's the man that counts and, just passing through the country, I prefer to be known as Gun-smoke."

"Gun-smoke it is!" replied the Colonel with a bow; but as he pocketed the bills he sighed. It was more money than he had seen for many a long day, and it would pay his debt at the store; but among gentlemen——"

"Now another thing," began Gun-smoke after he had tucked away the notes, "I'm going to ask you not to mention this deal of ours to anyone—otherwise Old Scorp will catch on. And if he ever hears that I'm buying up his notes I can kiss that money good-bye."

"Very well, suh," agreed Blood, "but my wife and daughter——"

"You can tell 'em," suggested Gun-smoke, "that you win it in a poker game. Only don't you play any poker. What I mean is, don't flash a roll and set people to talking——"

"I trust I understand," responded the Colonel grimly. "And I wish you the best of luck. But at the same time, young man, you're throwing away your money. You'll never beat Old Scorp Plunkett."

"You don't know my dad," answered Gun-smoke. "He's the smartest danged cowman in Texas."

CHAPTER XIII

A Horse-trade

A BLANK, lonely silence settled down over Blood's Canyon, and the cowboys who had ridden past to make eyes at Johnsie were conspicuous by their absence. Yet as two days passed and nothing whatever happened the Bloods relaxed their vigilance. Under cover of darkness the Colonel rode to his hounds, which had been starving as they bayed a lion; and when he returned with the lion-skin, after feeding the dogs the flesh, all fear of the Night Riders ceased.

The Colonel sat in the doorway, looking off down the canyon while he told long stories of the hunt; and while her mother did the housework and looked after the invalid, Johnsie slipped down to her garden in the creek bed. There within a massive fence, bull-strong and horse-high, long rows of radishes and crinkly green lettuce stretched out to delight the eye—and help mitigate their diet of straight beef. But at a whoop from the lower gate she came running like a deer and dashed panting into her room.

"Dandy's coming!" she gasped as she threw off her faded gingham and washed the grime from her hands; and Gun-smoke grumbled to himself. When he had come back there had been no changing of dresses, no frantic search after stockings and tight shoes; but now as Dandy McAllister rode up from the gate the house was in a furore of preparation. Hounds were kicked from under the bed, sun-bonnets whisked out of sight; and the Colonel, smoothing his beard, stood waiting in the doorway to welcome the honored guest.

"Well, well!" hailed McAllister as he rode up to the cabin. "How's the Colonel—say, I brought you a bottle!"

He spoke quickly in Spanish and Gun-smoke, craning his neck, spied the Stone-eater, bowing obsequiously. In one hand was a bottle of whisky and a box of cigars, while under his arm he bore a larger box, bulging temptingly with candy and fruits.

"Good morning, suh, good morning!" responded the Colonel heartily. "Well, Dandy, I'm sure glad to see you! How's everything down at Barcee?"

"O.K.," replied Dandy. "How's the Princess of Blood's Canyon. I'm hastening to pay my devoirs!"

He took the large box from the hands of his servant and started toward the door, but as he glanced in and saw Gun-smoke he stopped.

"Well, where'd *you* come from?" he burst out, staring incredulously. "I thought you'd gone to Las Vegas!"

"Done gone and come back again," answered Gun-smoke lightly. "Something mighty attractive about this canyon."

"My God, have you been shot again?" exclaimed Dandy in despair. "It's been rumored around you were dead."

"Slightly premature," observed Gun-smoke. "They figure on getting me later. But don't let me spoil your day."

He jerked his head towards the inner doorway, where Johnsie stood smiling, and Dandy made his bow. Then,

GUN-SMOKE

turning to Mrs. Blood, he bowed again and offered the box of fruit. But it was plain that Gun-smoke's presence had killed the joy of his visit and he eyed him uneasily as they talked. For he knew without more words that Gun-smoke had met the Night Riders and that their guns had given him his wounds. And, since they had failed to kill him, he knew beyond a doubt that the cabin in the canyon was watched.

"How's the garden?" he enquired as soon as politeness would permit it; and at a smile from Johnsie he accompanied her down the path while her mother bustled about getting dinner. As for the Colonel, though he opened the bottle, his thoughts were far away, and after fuming in silence he went out.

Gun-smoke moved in his bed and grumbled to himself as he felt his still-stiffened wound. He was an incubus—he was strictly in the way—and yet he could not go. From the doorway he caught the whiff of a corn-husk cigarette and as he lay there brooding there was a shuffle of footsteps and Juan Brabon peered in around the corner.

"*Buenos dias!*" greeted Gun-smoke. "Good morning, *Señor Come-piedras!*" And the Stone-eater beamed with joy.

"Ah, you speak Spanish!" he cried, standing bareheaded and bowing outside the door; but Gun-smoke shook his head.

"Only a few words," he replied haltingly, "but how is the stone-eating business?"

"*No hay*—there is none!" responded Brabon smiling broadly. "Since the Señor took to shooting swallows."

"That is well for you," observed Gun-smoke. "Otherwise your name might be One-eye."

A HORSE-TRADE

"I had thought of that, also," admitted the Stone-eater. "My daughter sends her thanks."

"For what?" demanded Gun-smoke bluffly.

"For driving El Queek away," he replied, and his keen eyes lighted up with triumph.

"It was nothing," said Gun-smoke; but the Stone-eater shrugged and tapped his shoulder significantly.

"Did he shoot you?" he enquired ingratiatingly.

"Quien sabe—who knows!" shrugged back Gun-smoke; and for a long time the old man stood silent. Then he bowed and took his leave.

"Many thanks!" he said, "from Lolita!" And with another smile he was gone.

There was an interval of silence and then from the kitchen Colonel Blood strode purposefully in.

"What have you ever done for Lolita?" he asked; and Gun-smoke looked up with a start.

"Nothing at all," he replied, for he could see the Colonel was angry; but at the answer Blood burst into a roar.

"Did that old man come in heah?" he demanded. "Did he dare to put his foot across my doorway? By the gods, if he had I'd kill him—do you know his daughter, Lolita?"

"W'y, yes," responded Gun-smoke but before he could go further Mrs. Blood came hurrying in.

"Please, Henry!" she begged. "Mr. McAllister is coming back! Do you want him and Johnsie to hear?"

"Him or anyone!" stormed the Colonel. "I tell you it's a damned outrage to bring that girl's father to my house. Is he——"

GUN-SMOKE

"Henry!" she cried, laying a hand on his arm. "Please hush, now—Dandy is our guest!"

She looked him in the eye and the Colonel subsided, though he continued to mutter in his beard.

"Oh, Mother!" called Johnsie from the foot of the hill, "Dandy says he has to go!"

"Let him go, then!" growled the Colonel but at a glance from his wife he remembered his duties as a host. Yet, brief as were his expressions of regret, they were hardly noted by the flustered Dandy. Some quarrel had taken place during their visit to the garden and Johnsie's eyes were big with tears; but she bore up bravely until her lover had left, then ran up the canyon and hid. The Colonel paced back and forth, drinking often from the bottle but scorning to smoke Dandy's cigars; and at last he too flung out of the house, leaving his wife to weep alone.

Gun-smoke looked on, saying nothing, but he knew in his heart that the Stone-eater was the cause of it all. His presence had constituted an insult, both to Johnsie and her parents, for it had brought up the wraith of Lolita. Yet why that should give offence was a mystery to Gun-smoke and he preferred to leave it so. To him Juan Brabon was a brave and loyal Mexican who ate stones from a spoon to please his master, and if Lolita had gone too far in her devotion to *El Patron* that also was not his affair. But nevertheless he suffered, for Johnsie avoided him; and her eyes were black with hate.

The next morning the militant Colonel rode down to Barcee and returned with his store bill, paid in full. That was his answer to Dandy McAllister, but it did not dry

A HORSE-TRADE

Johnsie's tears. Gun-smoke stood it for two days until his arm got a little stronger, then secretly he prepared to go.

First he cleaned and oiled his guns and got together his rigging, then he called Watch-eye often to the door; and one evening just at dusk, when no one was about, he stepped out, dragging his saddle.

"Watch-eye," he said as he slipped on the bridle, "we ain't wanted here, a-tall. Shall we beat it back to Texas, Old Socks?"

Watch-eye whickered and bobbed his head, champing his bit impatiently; and once more without farewells Gun-smoke drifted off down the canyon, but at the gate Watch-eye snorted and stopped. Gun-smoke ducked, for the fear of the Night Riders was upon him; but it was Johnsie, leaning over the bars. Not since her quarrel with Dandy had she given him more than a glance, but now she regarded him intently.

"Well—on my way," he announced; and in the gathering gloom he saw her lips twist to a smile.

"Running away again, eh?" she said.

"Yep, making a sneak," he admitted. "Trying to side-step them Night Riders. Much obliged for taking me in."

He reined up to the bars and she let them down in silence, then patted Watch-eye's neck as he passed.

"Look out!" warned Gun-smoke. "My Lord, that horse will bite you!" But Johnsie only laughed.

"You will not, will you Watch-eye?" she wheedled and laid her face against his broad cheek.

"What the devil?" accused Gun-smoke, jerking his horse's

head away, "have you been feeding Watch-eye sugar? I told you to leave him alone!"

"Now you quit abusing him!" she flared up indignantly. "I declare, it's a shame—a nice horse like that, being yanked around by some brute."

"Brute—nothing!" retorted Gun-smoke; and then, as her voice broke, he stepped down and stood beside her. "Never mind, Johnsie," he said, "I didn't mean to hurt him. But he's mine—can't you understand?"

"No!" she cried rebelliously. "All you think about is that horse—and sneaking off without saying good-bye. And now I know you'll never come back, because Dad would kill you, sure. But oh, well, you're all the same!"

"Who's all the same?" he demanded contentiously; and then his voice softened for her face was twisted with pain. "I'm sorry, Johnsie," he said, "but I know you just hated me—so I thought the best thing was to go."

"I do not!" she denied. "It's Dandy McAllister I hate. Did you see that Lolita? Was she there?"

"Sure," acknowledged Gun-smoke, and something within him gave warning for him to beware.

"Was she—pretty?" she asked at last.

"Sure," he returned, "for a Mex."

"I heard," she went on accusingly, "that she gave you a kiss when you drove that Quick Murrah out of town. Is that true? Did you let her kiss you?"

She was breathing hard now but he faced her imperturbably.

"Sure did," he admitted. "Couldn't help it."

"You could too!" she declared, contemptuously. "But you

A HORSE-TRADE

men are all the same. You make love to some Mexican girl and then you come around and——"

"Not me!" broke in Gun-smoke resolutely.

"Well, then—Dandy!" she snapped. "And I just hate him for it—and for humiliating me before my own people. But Daddy went down and paid every cent he owed—he had the money hid, all the time. Oh, why didn't he do it before?"

She sighed wearily and turned away and Gun-smoke shuffled his feet. They were getting on dangerous ground.

"Listen, Johnsie," he said, "what's the use of blaming me for what McAllister has done? Haven't we always been good friends? Well, why not shake hands now and say good-bye like folks, instead of giving me hell?"

He held out his hand and she took it, reluctantly; but Gun-smoke did not let it go. At the touch of her hand something strange swept over him and the evening star swam in the sky.

"Johnsie," he said softly, "I'm going away now; but if you said so I might come back. And not under a flag but like a sure-enough hombre—with just one name, like a good piano. I know I've been onery, but I think a lot of you, Johnsie—I'd give a horse for one kiss!"

She snatched her hand away and stood glaring up at him—then she laughed, a hard, hurt laugh.

"So you're just like the rest," she observed. "And you'd give a horse for one kiss!"

Her voice was mocking now but Gun-smoke was dead in earnest.

"Sure would!" he repeated. "And I'd always remember it. I think a lot of you, Johnsie."

"Well, we'll see!" she challenged. "You'd give a horse for one kiss, eh? All right—take the kiss and give me Watch-eye!"

She raised her lips with a swift, alluring smile but Gun-smoke turned as if from a blow.

"Not much!" he stated. "You don't git Watch-eye. I'd just as soon give my right arm."

"Ah, that's it!" she retorted. "I knew you were lying. You think more of Watch-eye than me."

"No-o," he answered slowly, "but I'll tell you how it is. Me and Watch-eye are pardners—he's like folks."

"You can keep him," she laughed. "I was only joking, anyway. I just wanted to see what a man would do if I took him at his word."

"I'll tell you what I'll do," offered Gun-smoke eagerly. "I'll give you Watch-eye's brother. But not for no trading kiss—I want a real good one, so you and me can be friends."

"We can be friends without that," she answered at last. "And I don't trade kisses, Mistuh Gun-smoke."

"No, I know you don't," he burst out. "That's why I like you, Johnsie. But if I'd bring you a horse like Watch-eye don't you reckon you could give me just one?"

"No, I couldn't!" she stormed. "You're just like Dandy McAllister! He thinks because he's rich he can get anything. But a woman——"

"No, I'm not, now!" he flared back, "and don't you never think it. You can keep that line of talk for him. And I'll bet you a hundred dollars if you saw Watch-eye's brother you'd trade me a kiss quick as that!"

A HORSE-TRADE

He snapped his fingers contemptuously and swung into the saddle and Johnsie glared up at him, raging.

"You can go to Lolita for that kiss!" she scoffed.

"I don't have to," he answered after a silence that made her flinch; and he reined Watch-eye into the trail. But Johnsie did not weaken.

He jabbed the spurs into Watch-eye as he turned his head to look, then looked back himself and sighed. But Johnsie did not speak—she stood waiting by the bars and his pride would not let him return.

"Good-bye!" he called as the darkness closed in about him; and Johnsie took a step, and stopped.

"Good-bye, yourse'f!" she answered back scornfully; but when he was gone she bit her lip. Then, leaning against the bars, she gazed out into the night, which had swallowed him up in its murk. Would he come back, this man without a name? Or had she lost him forever? She stirred uneasily and an unbidden tear welled up and rolled down her cheek. Then, far out on the plain, a line of fire stabbed the night and she heard the muffled pop of a gun. Three jets of fire flashed defiantly back and in the silence that followed she heard the distant drumming of hoof-beats. It was the Night Riders—they had been watching—they knew! And even then her lover was fighting for his life.

"Oh, Gun-smoke!" she cried. "I'm sorry! I'm sorry!" But Gun-smoke did not hear.

CHAPTER XIV

A Present for Johnsie

SUMMER came in its full tide and far out over the plains the thunder-caps rode up, big with rain. Long trailers reached down and touched the parched earth, the storm-clouds turned black and spread; then the wind whipped around and blew the other way and clouds and fury passed. But though Johnsie watched the plain no pinto horse appeared, bearing Gun-smoke, the man without a name. Perhaps even then, somewhere in that vastness, his bones lay bleaching on the prairie. And he had offered a horse for one kiss!

At thought of his effrontery Johnsie stamped her foot angrily, but at the memory of his words she sighed. He had always laughed before, exchanging quip for merry quip, but at their parting he had spoken from the heart. And even as he waited the Night Riders were laying an ambush to kill him. What a mockery that she, waylaying him at the gate, had delivered him into their hands. He had known the need of haste but he had lingered for one kiss—and she had told him to go to Lolita!

As the days passed white-topped wagons appeared on the horizon, moving slowly in from the east. It was the settlers, pushing on ahead of the railroad to look out the promised

A PRESENT FOR JOHNSIE

land. Johnsie could ride out freely now, for Quick Murrah and his warriors had other work, nearer at hand. Where before they had harassed one homesteader they now had a hundred to intimidate, and more and more came every day.

They were boomers, men with vision, who saw in each valley a farmstead with fenced fields and cows. But Zim Plunkett saw only the trouble they would cause him and he moved them with ruthless haste. There was no time given for the newcomers to take root—no sooner had they camped than a rider was upon them with a warning to leave at dawn. And at dusk, if that warning was not obeyed, the Night Riders descended like furies.

Disguised perhaps as Indians, or wearing the high hats of Mexicans, they ran off the settlers' horses and cows; and only when the homesteaders had promised to move on would Zim Plunkett restore their stock. Some resisted, but it was easier to drift on into the west—and if they stayed the Night Riders struck. Cabins were burned, wagons destroyed, horses driven into the hills to be picked up by the hostile Utes; but still they came seeking, for the railroad was pressing west and the surveyors were setting their stakes.

Strange men came and went through the broad plaza of Barcee, where the white stakes of a townsite had been set; and one morning from her lookout, where she watched the trail below, Johnsie Blood spied a pinto horse. A tall man wearing a Texas hat was riding him towards Portales, and at sight of him her heart almost stopped. For he was black, like Watch-eye, with the same vivid white markings; and the man who bestrode him rode like Gun-smoke.

Johnsie leapt up and waved her hand but as the cavalcade

GUN-SMOKE

came nearer she saw it was not Watch-eye, not Gun-smoke. This horse had a galaxy of white stars on his hip, his face was not painted like Watch-eye's; and the man had a beard that gleamed in the sun like the tawny mane of a lion. Two cowboys rode behind him, each dragging a pack-animal, and she caught the glint of guns on their saddles. They were cowmen, passing through to look out the land, and at the fork of the trail they halted.

Instantly Johnsie jumped up from her lookout on the high point, and when they turned in she ran for the gate. Perhaps they brought news from Gun-smoke. But as they approached her heart sank for they were strangers, and heavily armed, and the man in the lead eyed her grimly.

"Good morning," she faltered as he bowed and tipped his hat. "When I waved to you down there I—I thought you were a friend of mine."

"No ma'am," he answered briefly, though with a quizzical smile. "I'm a stranger in these parts. Does Colonel Blood live up this canyon?"

"Yes—I'm his daughter," she responded eagerly; but the big man did not give her his news.

"We'll go up and pay him a visit," he said to his two companions and they rode on up to the house.

At the loud challenge of the hounds the Colonel peered out the doorway, then stepped back and picked up his gun. It was a habit he had developed, but when the stranger held up his hand Blood silenced the dogs and came out.

"Good morning, gentlemen," he greeted. "I am Colonel Henry Blood, suh!" And he bowed to the big man in front.

A PRESENT FOR JOHNSIE

"Enright is my name," he responded amiably. "I'm a cattle-buyer, from Texas."

"Oh, a cattle-buyer, eh?" smiled the Colonel. "Well, you've come to the wrong place, I'm afraid. But get down, suh—get down, gentlemen—you're very welcome, I'm sure. Ah, Mrs. Blood—allow me to present Mistuh Enright."

The two hard-faced cowboys sat their mounts in stony silence, rolling their eyes now and then at the hills, but the cattle-buyer stepped inside. The Colonel called for glasses and produced a bottle of whisky, then waited for his guest to speak.

"Have you any steers to sell?" enquired Enright with Northern directness. "I've just bought three thousand head from Mr. McAllister, to be delivered the first of July."

"Well, yes and no, suh," replied the Colonel gloomily. "I have steers, but not to sell. And, not to put too fine a point on the matter, the reason is I can't give title. The steers are mine, you understand, but they've been appropriated by Zim Plunkett, the owner of the ZIPs. My brand, suh, is the XL-Bar."

"I've seen that iron, back in Texas," nodded the cattle buyer. "What kind of a man is this Plunkett."

"He's a dadblasted cow-thief!" blared the Colonel angrily; and without further prompting he plunged into the story of his unfortunate dealings with Plunkett.

"Well, well," observed the stranger, "that certainly was hard luck. I won't buy any XL-Bars from Plunkett."

"Or any other brand!" raged the Colonel. "He stole every cow that he's got. And if the cows were stolen property,

GUN-SMOKE

the natural increase belongs to the owners who were defrauded by his worthless notes."

"That sounds reasonable, too," agreed Enright. "But at the same time, I believe I'll pay him a call. The railroad has been constructed as far as Texmex, and the cattle business is bound to pick up."

"Keep away from Portales!" warned the Colonel vehemently. "It's a deadfall—you're liable to be robbed. And don't buy a single head from Plunkett—unless, suh, which I doubt, you desire to purchase stolen property."

"A clean brand and a bill of sale is all I ask," returned the cattle-buyer. "That's the law, and it satisfies the inspectors. But at the same time, Colonel Blood, I'll remember your advice, and I thank you for the information."

He shook hands to go, but as he stepped out the door he found Johnsie anxiously awaiting him. While they talked she had been looking at the pinto.

"That's a nice horse you've got there," she spoke up boldly; and the cattle-buyer exchanged glances with his cowboys.

"Think so?" he answered; and she nodded defiantly, for her father was regarding her sternly.

"My daughter," he volunteered. "Mistuh Enright. Now run into the house," he added.

"I was wondering," went on Johnsie, ignoring her father's nod, "where you got a horse like that."

"Well," observed Enright, as his cowboys began to grin, "in a co'te of law I'd decline to answer that question, on the ground that I might incriminate myself. Do you happen to know the animal?"

A PRESENT FOR JOHNSIE

"No," she answered, "but—did you get him from a young man named Gun-smoke?"

"I believe that was his name," admitted the cattle-buyer. "He was a big, strapping fellow that I met on the road, the other side of Texmex; and when I told him I was coming to this part of the country he gave me this horse—for you."

"For me!" she cried, and before her parents could speak she ran and gave the pinto a hug. "Oh, he's *such* a nice horse!" she exclaimed.

"No, Johnsie," reproved her mother, "you mustn't take on so. Because of course you can't accept him."

"Why not?" she demanded rebelliously. "And oh, I just love him! Please, Mother—don't you think it's all right?"

"I might say," put in the cattle-buyer, "that the young man seemed very anxious, and he wouldn't take 'No' for an answer. I hope, Madam, there's nothing wrong?"

"Oh, no," spoke up Mrs. Blood, "only I'd prefer, under the circumstances, that my daughter shouldn't keep the horse."

"The young man," explained the Colonel, "was a guest in our house. But on both occasions he left between two days—and he neglected to give his name."

"On the dodge, eh?" smiled Enright. "Well, he looked it. One arm was in a sling, he had a bullet-hole through his hat and—"

"Oh, they tried to kill him—again!" broke in Johnsie; but she was silenced by a glance from Blood.

"This young man," he said, "was shot at Portales, after an altercation with Zim Plunkett, and he came quite by

GUN-SMOKE

accident to my house. Then he left and two days later he returned, wounded again—as he claimed, by Zim Plunkett's men. He was a natural-born fighter and I couldn't help but admire his courage, but it's a custom among gentlemen——"

"Oh, now Daddy!" wailed Johnsie, *"why* can't I keep the horse? You know Gun-smoke wasn't a thief! He was just passing through and—and I know he was a gentleman, only he didn't want to give his name!"

"No!" thundered the Colonel, "and he didn't want to stop and thank us for our hospitality, either! It's a custom among gentlemen——"

"But the Night Riders were after him!" she pleaded. "If they saw him shaking hands and saying good-bye——"

"He sent word," broke in Enright, "that he hoped to come back and thank you for your kindness, Colonel!"

"Oh, he did, eh?" observed the Colonel, suddenly mollified. "Well then, Amy, under the circumstances——"

"No, Henry!" spoke up Mrs. Blood firmly. "Johnsie is not a child now and——"

"Oh, but Mother!" protested Johnsie. "Of course I'm not a child! And I'm—just—going—to keep—this—horse!"

She buried her face in the pinto's mane and burst into such a storm of weeping that the Colonel turned appealingly to his wife.

"Let her keep him," he said. "I'll attend to Mistuh Gun-smoke, if he enters my door again!"

"Well——" began Mrs. Blood and Johnsie sprang forward and kissed her on both cheeks at once.

A PRESENT FOR JOHNSIE

"I'll let *you* ride him, too!" she promised and her mother's strained face relaxed.

"Very well, Mistuh Enright," she bowed. "My daughter may accept the horse. But if Mistuh Gun-smoke comes back——"

"I'll attend to him!" promised the Colonel, "personally!"

The cattle-buyer smiled and unsaddled the gentle pinto, which had nothing of the fighting mien of Watch-eye; but as he transferred his rigging to one of the pack animals a sudden thought came to Johnsie.

"Mistuh Enright," she began, beckoning him anxiously aside, "did—did Gun-smoke send any message? Did he say why he sent the horse?"

"W'y, no, I reckon not," answered the cattle-buyer as he scratched his thatch of light hair. "But now you speak of it I believe he did mention that he'd be back later on, for his pay."

"His pay!" repeated Johnsie, in dismay. "Why, what did he mean by that?"

"I don't know," he responded, "but if you don't want to accept the horse——"

"Oh, I'll accept him," she answered tremulously, "only——"

"I'd be glad to keep him, myself!" he ended.

"No!" she cried. "You can't have him—he's mine! Only—well, maybe I'll give him back," she said.

CHAPTER XV

THE ROYAL BENGAL TIGER

JOHNSIE did not tell her mother that in a reckless moment she had offered to trade a kiss for a horse—a kiss, that is, for Watch-eye. Nor did she ever mention Gun-smoke's brusque refusal, and his offer of Watch-eye's brother in his stead. Because as sure as she was living she knew that this strange horse was own brother to Gun-smoke's pinto. But Gun-smoke would never come back!

Yet if he did, if he came, what answer could she give—for now she would never give up Star-dust. She had named him that herself, for the white stars on his coal-black coat and the great star that was blazed on his forehead; and every morning at dawn she ran out and called him for fear that he might be stolen. Behind its bull-tight fence her garden lay neglected, for Johnsie was mounted now and scouring the plains or riding with her father to the hounds. The close canyon no longer penned her in, shutting her up like the walls of a jail—she was free and Star-dust was her playmate.

There were no long days of waiting for Dandy to call, no hungering for news of the great outside world or of the wagon-trains passing by. Before she had been afoot, except for a scrubby pony, but now she was mounted like a queen.

THE ROYAL BENGAL TIGER

And what sweet revenge it was, when she passed Dandy in Barcee, to see him eyeing her horse. Let him go back to his Mexican girl—he must know in his heart that Gunsmoke had given her Star-dust. And a man who, for a present, could bestow horses like her pinto was far from being a vagabond. He was a man who, back in Texas, would have a father and a name—and something told her that name was Enright.

The man who had brought her this fine horse from Gunsmoke was like him—he had his slow smile! And besides, Gun-smoke had mentioned the name of Bill Enright as a substitute for his *nom-de-guerre*. From the depths of her memory the name had risen up as she had pondered on Gun-smoke and his past, and in a flash she had put two and two together, meanwhile making a new world of her own.

In it the outlaw Gun-smoke was no longer a renegade, he was son to this big cattle-buyer with the tawny yellow beard and the two cowboys who rode at his back. They had met, not by accident, but by appointment at Texmex, and somewhere in the broad prairie beyond lay the mansion that both called home. Pinto horses roamed wide pastures, cattle drifted across the plains; and Gun-smoke the fugitive owned an honored name—back there in the land of her dreams.

But time passed and, though wagons came through by the score, neither Gun-smoke nor Enright the cattle-buyer appeared, and the dreamland faded away. The days lagged at last in spite of her jaunts with Star-dust and when Dandy McAllister came riding up the canyon Johnsie greeted him

GUN-SMOKE

with her old-time smile. For youth cannot wait—it must live.

"Big news!" he called as he waved his hand gaily, "the circus is coming to Texmex! The elephant, the camel and everything! Want to go over and take in the sights?"

"Oh, an elephant!" she exclaimed rapturously. "I've never even seen one! And think of the lions and tigers!"

"The whole ZIP outfit is going—to a man! So you don't need to worry about your cabin!"

Dandy addressed this to the Colonel, who was shaking his head bodingly, and suddenly the contagion swept on.

"Oh, let's go, Henry!" appealed his wife, "you can hire some man to stay here."

"I'll send up two!" offered Dandy. "But folks, you've just got to go! It's the opening of the railroad and the whole country will be there; but I've got two Texas gunmen that don't dare cross the line, so they'll stay here and guard your ranch. Hey, Johnsie—are you game to go?"

"If Mother does," she answered demurely and the Colonel nodded to his wife.

"You go, Amy," he said, "and take Johnsie to the circus. I'll stay and guard this cabin, myself—I've no confidence in the integrity of these gunmen!"

"Well, you and Johnsie, then!" Dandy appealed to Mrs. Blood. "I'll hook up my buckboard and a span of good horses —but I've got to have company, that's all!"

He glanced admiringly at Johnsie, who answered with half-veiled eyes; and three days later to the patter of well-shod hoofs they went dashing down the road towards Texmex.

THE ROYAL BENGAL TIGER

They passed ranch-wagons filled with Mexican families, escorted by swart vaqueros; there were Indians in their savage finery; and many a white-topped wagon which had brought some new settler now carried him back to Texmex. It was a Fourth of July and Pioneer Day combined. It was Circus Day—and the opening of the railroad.

The long lines of polished steel ended abruptly at the Texas line, like the outthrust fingers of some distant monster, reaching out from the distant east. Thus far it had thrust, and while it rested and gained new strength a town sprang up over-night. The track itself ran down the middle of the street, which was wide enough to swing a bull-team; and from false-front saloons drunken cowboys and railroaders shouted challenges and invitations across the way.

From the shipping-pens beyond the town there came the roar of range bulls and the deep, organ-notes of lowing steers. For Texmex was a cow-town, where thousands of head of cattle were shipped to the markets of the East. Other industries there were none, except those which gave pleasure to the cowboys and layers of tracks; and to get their money quicker a score of saloons and dance-halls had sprung up on both sides of the track. But beyond these, out on the prairie, rose the high-towering circus tent, with its flags and flaunting banners; and as the opening hour approached all lesser joys were abandoned to gaze on the elephant and the lion.

Johnsie gasped with delight at the mere sight of the tent, which covered fully an acre of ground; the barkers at the side-shows held her spell-bound; but even with all these wonders and with Dandy at her side, she looked through

GUN-SMOKE

the crowd for Gun-smoke. It was not right, of course, since Johnsie was Dandy's guest and he a most attentive squire of dames; but the memory of Gun-smoke made her forget that small disloyalty—he had said he was coming back. And if these broad plains held him he would be there, for all the world had come. Yet nowhere did she see man or horse. For Watch-eye would be with him, and who even there could overlook that proud head with its glassy, questioning eyes?

In the hurly-burly of the first opening the big tent was filled in no time. Johnsie could hear the cracking of whips and the loud guffaws of the crowd as they witnessed the antics of the clowns; but the side-show with its animals held her fascinated with wonder and they lingered in the long, outer tent. Here, still mounted on their wagons, the great cats and lions lay glaring out through the bars; but the king of them all was Rajah, the Royal Bengal tiger.

He lay stretched full length within his ornate cage, his sleek hide gorgeously patterned with black and orange stripes, his yellow eyes fixed on the crowd. Johnsie gazed and hurried on to where the elephants stood swaying, their feet securely manacled with chains. But when, an hour later, she turned back towards Rajah's cage she stopped short and clutched her mother's arm. For there, surrounded by cowboys, stood Quick Murrah himself—his eyes on Rajah's tawny hide.

"Say, Mister," he called to the grim-faced attendant who stood wearily surveying the crowd, "how much do you want for that animile?"

THE ROYAL BENGAL TIGER

"He ain't for sale," answered the attendant politely. "This is Rajah, the finest tiger in captivity."

"Yes, I know it is," bawled Murrah, who was feeling his liquor, "that's why I want to buy him, my friend. I want to use his hide to make me a pair of shaps. So don't be bashful—name yore price!"

"He ain't for sale!" repeated the circus-man shortly; and Murrah ripped out an oath.

"Hyer!" he said, whipping out a roll of bills. "What do you think I am, a cheap sport? I'm flush, understand? And I want what I want! Put a price on yore Bengal tiger!"

The attendant gave a signal which brought the canvas-men running with the long tent-staves they used in a fight, then he turned to the abusive cowboy.

"This animal ain't for sale—at no price!" he announced. "Can't you learn to take 'No' for an answer?"

"No!" answered Murrah, cursing wickedly. "I'm going to have them shaps—understand? Come on, boys, let's smoke this bunch up!"

He led the way out of the tent and the circus-men thought no more of it, but as the main show started up and the crowd thinned out there was a clatter of flying hoofs outside the door. Then twenty mounted cowboys came dashing through the entrance and Quick Murrah let out a yell. He was drunk and his pistols were smoking. With an answering whoop the ZIP cowboys closed in behind him and they charged down to where Rajah stood glaring.

"He's my meat!" yelped Murrah, setting his horse up in front of the tiger; and with three lightning shots he laid him dead in his blood and jumped down to tear off his hide.

Circus-men came running wildly, the crowd broke and ran; but twenty shooting outlaws were banked up before the cage where their leader was plying his knife. With ruthless skill he stretched out the tawny creature and skinned him like a slaughtered beef. He worked fast, for the canvasmen were swarming to the attack, and the Texas Rangers were in town; but not until the hide was neatly stripped away did he heed the shouts of his friends.

"Hyer it is, boys!" he yelled, leaping up into his saddle and spreading the skin over his legs. "The finest pair of shaps in New Mexico!"

He spurred his horse into the lead, the gorgeous hide of the tiger almost dragging the ground on both sides. Then, whipping out his pistols he charged straight for the entrance and the circus-men broke and ran. Outside the big canvas he wheeled and circled the tents, his wild cowboys spurring at his back. There was a rattle of spitting six-shooters, a chorus of taunting whoops; and then like a flash they were gone. Two men on galloping ponies were heading out from town and Quick Murrah knew them—they were Rangers. But the skin of Rajah, the Royal Bengal tiger, hung trailing across his saddle as he fled.

CHAPTER XVI

ZIM PLUNKETT MEETS HIS NEMESIS

ALL that summer and fall, in his gorgeous tiger-skin shaps, Quick Murrah rode forth to harry the nesters who had settled on Plunkett's range. There was no law to protect them now—no pretense of law, since the sheriff and his deputies had fled—and the Night Riders did their worst; but with the first warm days of spring new settlers moved in and Old Scorp saw he was whipped. Against the land-hunger of these people there was no recourse save one, and the Night Riders could not kill them all.

They came on like a great wave, a white tide of covered wagons that flowed like water down the road, and as the leaders settled down on the deserted homesteads along the creek-beds Zim Plunkett called off his men. It was a wave, and like a wave it would pass. The west still beckoned and when the wagon-trains had passed the settlers who remained could be moved. So he loopholed his houses, barricaded the strong gate and rounded up his steers to sell.

At the lure of that much beef on the hoof the cattle-buyers came in swarms, but as they rode through the herd and saw the vented Texas brands they paltered and turned away. There was a cattle inspector at Texmex who could neither be bought nor bluffed, and Plunkett insisted upon range delivery. And who, knowing his name, would put money in Old Scorp's hands while the cattle were still in his pasture? He looked on in surly silence as the buyers came and went, for Money was Plunkett's particular god.

But the price of cattle was up and one morning there came to Portales a buyer that Plunkett knew. He was a big man with a tawny beard and the year before he had bought from McAllister, for cash. It was Enright, of Enright and Valentine. Behind him rode ten cowboys where before there had been but two; and that alone spoke of money, for every man was heavily armed. They were hard men and at the gate they sat their horses in watchful silence while the Boss stepped down and shook hands.

"Good morning, Mr. Plunkett," he greeted. "Morning, suh—how are you, Mr. Murrah? I was just riding through and I thought I'd stop over and enquire how you hold your steers."

"I hold 'em cheap, sir, cheap!" spoke up Plunkett belligerently. "But these dadrammed cattle-buyers are afraid to touch 'em, on account of that inspector at Texmex."

"I see," nodded Enright, glancing up the broad valley where the fat steers grazed by the thousand, "they're certainly looking fine. What price do you put on them, Mr. Plunkett?"

"Wall!" jockeyed Plunkett, "I'm jest waiting for the snow to melt. Believe I'll drive 'em north, when the trail opens, and put 'em on the market in Denver."

"That's a long drive," observed Enright, "and them steers are mighty fat. You'll lose lots of them, over the mountain."

"Hell! Make me a bid then!" yapped Plunkett. "Don't I know that Denver trail?"

ZIM PLUNKETT MEETS HIS NEMESIS

"I'll give you twenty dollars, round," offered the cattle-buyer promptly, "for three-year-old steers and better. And I'll take all you've got," he added.

"You will!" exclaimed Plunkett, hardly believing his ears. "But how about the pay?" he demanded.

"Well," smiled Enright, "you know the country, Mr. Plunkett. I'm not carrying that money around in my vest pocket. But on the day you deliver them steers at Texmex I'll have the cash in the bank. All I ask is a clean brand and a bill of sale. I'll take a chance on the rest."

"Umph-umm!" objected Plunkett. "Range delivery—right hyer. I've got enemies over in Texas and they're liable to do me dirt. Range delivery, and the steers are yores."

"I'll buy 'em my way or not at all," stated Enright. "I'll accept 'em at the Texas line. You and your cowboys can drive 'em over and hold 'em outside the town——"

"Range delivery!" croaked Plunkett. "That's final."

"I'll give you twenty-two dollars," offered Enright. "And I'll take every steer you've got that carries a straight earmark and brand. But you'll deliver them, Mr. Plunkett, at the line."

"You'll take 'em all?" repeated Plunkett, his crafty eyes gleaming. "No matter what the brand? You know, Mr. Enright, I had some trouble, back in Texas—them Texas brands go with the rest?"

"Any brand!" agreed Enright, "that hasn't been worked over. A blotched brand would be turned back anywhere."

"Gimme twenty-four dollars round and the steers are yores!" bargained Plunkett. "I'm wore out, waiting for a sale."

"Twenty-two!" answered Enright. "And it's distinctly understood that I'll accept delivery at the railroad."

"No, by grab!" yelped Plunkett. "Thar's some ketch in this, Quick. He's trying to take an advantage!"

"Mebbe so," returned Murrah, cocking his head at the ten cowboys, "but I reckon we can protect you, Uncle. And them twenty thousand steers will shore bring a lot of money at twenty-two dollars a head!"

"How much, Quick? How much?" pleaded the old man anxiously. "Git a big piece of paper and figger it out fer me—I ain't very much at book-learnin'!"

Murrah glanced at him pityingly, for the old cattle-man was barely able to sign his name; then, wetting a stub pencil, he figured thoughtfully on a board and opened his eyes at the total.

"Four hundred and forty thousand dollars!" he announced and Old Scorp stood staring at the ground.

"That's a lot of money," he said.

"Yes, it's nigh onto half a million dollars," returned Murrah and glanced significantly at his men. They had crowded out of the saloon and massed themselves behind him, their evil eyes fixed on Enright; but at the announcement of the price he had offered for their cattle a murmur went through the crowd.

"How the hell can he pay it?" exclaimed one of them incredulously, but Quick Murrah silenced him with a look.

"He'll pay," he said. "Ever hear of Enright and Valentine? All right, then—they've got the cash."

"You bet we have," agreed Enright. "And we pay on

ZIM PLUNKETT MEETS HIS NEMESIS

the nail, every time. The minute the last steer is tallied through the chutes Mr. Plunkett will get his money."

"By grab, Quick," shrilled Plunkett, "it don't seem reasonable! I want to sell them steers but——"

"Well, you'd better take him up, then," advised Murrah, "before the gentleman changes his mind."

"I—I know!" quavered Plunkett, "but they's a ketch in this, somewhar——"

"What's the matter?" demanded Murrah. "Don't you reckon you'll git yore money? I'll collect it—don't worry about that."

He slapped his pistol as he spoke and a grin passed over the crowd, for they knew he could make his word good; but Old Scorp stood gazing at the ground. In education he was a child compared to most of these men, but the shrewd dealings of a lifetime had sharpened his wits beyond theirs. He knew that something was wrong.

"I—I'll haf to think this over," he said at last; and Quick Murrah grabbed him by the arm.

"Heah!" he burst out arrogantly. "You owe me money, savvy? You owe all us boys our back pay. Now don't sit around and let this chance slip by. You take him up—understand?"

Plunkett looked at him searchingly, his grey eyebrows drawn down, his iron jaw set to resist; but something in Quick's eyes bade the master beware and he nodded his head with a sigh.

"All right," he agreed. "I'll take it, Mr. Enright. But the man never lived that could hornswaggle me, and I want that money in my hand."

GUN-SMOKE

"You'll get it," answered Enright. "Every dollar that's coming to you. And you can start those steers right now!"

He shook hands perfunctorily with the master of Portales, and again with his fighting boss; then, mounting his horse, he rode quietly out the gate and headed for distant Texmex. The trap had been set, the wary fox lured in—but when it was sprung, what then?

Huge herds of steers began to drift across the plains heading east towards the Texas line, and in order to make sure that no tricks were played Scorp Plunkett took all of his men. Never before had these warriors taken the trail together, and the enmity among them was strong; but as the great herds moved in and were counted through the chutes old grudges and quarrels were forgotten. Half a million dollars was falling into their hands—for Old Scorp, after all, was but one man. He was the master but they were seventy men.

But a hard life had taught Plunkett to trust no one but himself and those who were in his power. He saw the treason spreading, the black treachery that raised its head at thought of the money to be paid; and as the last steer was counted and driven to the pens he beckoned Quick Murrah to one side.

"Quick," he said, "you know me and I know you. I want you to he'p collect this money. But thar's no use getting it if them half-kiote whelps are going to take it away."

"Leave 'em to me," promised Quick, "and the first dog that yips I'll attend to his case with this."

He patted the pistol that hung at his hip and the old man nodded grimly. He knew that Quick could shoot.

ZIM PLUNKETT MEETS HIS NEMESIS

"Now another thing," he said, speaking low. "I don't trust this man, Enright, at all. He's too agreeable—they's a ketch in this, somewhar. You tell Ed and John I want 'em to come with us, and at the first crooked move you shoot."

"Aw, sho, sho!" soothed Murrah, "what makes you so spooky, Uncle? That's Enright, of Enright and Valentine. Every month of the year they buy that many cows. Ain't he got the money in the bank?"

"So he says," quavered Plunkett, "but I don't trust him, nohow. He's been too good-natured and obligin'. He's got a hold-out on me somewhar and I want you to watch him. And the first bobble he makes—you shoot!"

"Yes, and bring down the Rangers on my neck!" sneered Murrah. "This don't call for no shooting, and I know it. You're brave as hell with some other feller's neck—now listen to what I say. We'll go in thar, savvy, and Ed and John will go with us; and jest knowing my name for quick shooting, and so forth, Mr. Enright will give you yore money. He's got some understanding with that inspector, I tell ye—that's how come they passed those brands. He's made a mint of money on them cattle, the way it stands— what for would he hold out yore pay?"

"I don't trust him," complained Plunkett, "and you remember what I say. If he holds out my money, you kill him!"

"He ain't held it out yet," answered Quick Murrah viciously; but he beckoned over Ed and John.

They were the Big Three, the fighting Triumvirate, whose ready guns more than once had awed the rank and file of the Night Riders. For to kill one was to kill all

GUN-SMOKE

or go down fighting, and no one cared to take the chance. They rode up in silence to where Enright and the inspector were signing the last of their papers and as Old Scorp glanced back he was mightily heartened, for the Murrahs were men he could trust. They alone of all his warriors had the intelligence to remain loyal, and in return he paid them well.

"Well, gentlemen," announced Enright, "here's the tally on those steers—twenty-five thousand, eight hundred and eighty-eight. All correct, eh—it's the inspector's own count. All right then, we'll have a drink first and go over to the bank."

"I don't drink," replied Plunkett contrarily, "and I don't want my men to drink, until I git that thar money in my hands. How much does it come to, Quick?"

"Never mind!" snapped Murrah. "Have a drink with the gentleman. You must think he's trying to rob you!"

"No!" spoke up Enright, "the drinking can wait, then. I've made a good buy and I'm ready to pay the money." And he turned his horse towards town.

He rode alone, except for the sanitary inspector, and as that official quit them at the first saloon door Quick Murrah looked after him wistfully. He was a man who fought best when he was drunk. But Enright, the jovial cattle-buyer, was glum and silent now and Quick cursed under his breath.

"The old walloper!" he grumbled to his brothers. "Done got that buyer good and sore!"

The Stockmen and Drovers Bank stood just across the Texas line and as Murrah passed the monument in the middle of the street he glanced up and down the sidewalk.

ZIM PLUNKETT MEETS HIS NEMESIS

Since he had shot up the circus and killed the Bengal tiger he had stayed on the New Mexico side, but the broad board walk was deserted. The street in fact was empty, suspiciously empty; but the rumble of many voices from the neighboring saloon explained the absence of the crowd. Yet as they stepped into the big, stone bank and found it also empty Quick glanced at his brothers and frowned. Something was wrong—he believed it, now.

"Here's the tally," spoke up Enright, turning abruptly to Quick and placing a sheet of paper in his hand. "Now you figure out the total at twenty-two dollars a head and we'll have this business over with."

He stood facing Zim Plunkett, who glared back at him balefully; and as a customer came in Plunkett whirled like a tiger, but Quick Murrah barely looked up.

"By grab," he said at last, "that's an awful lot of money, unless my figgerin' is wrong." He ran over his figures again and Enright waited patiently—and at that moment two more customers came in. They were cowmen and wore pistols in their belts, but Plunkett was watching Quick.

"How much do you figger it?" he asked and Murrah slapped down the paper.

"Five hundred and sixty-nine thousand, five hundred and thirty-six dollars!" he announced, and glanced up defiantly at Enright.

"That's right," he acknowledged quietly. "Shore does credit to your schooling, Mr. Murrah. And now, Mr. Plunkett, if you'll step in here I'll count you out your money."

He pointed towards the door of the directors' room, but

Old Scorp shook his head. He was dazed, but his hunch was still strong.

"You bring the money out," he said cautiously.

"All right," assented Enright; and with a grim, twisted smile he stepped in and closed the door.

Silence followed and Zim Plunkett, standing surrounded by his gunmen, stared about like a strange, frightened cat. Men were coming and going now, the cashiers were cashing checks and a line had formed at one window; and he could not but observe that every customer of this bank had a pistol in his coat or belt.

"My Gawd, Quick," he whispered, "go and knock on that door. Thar's something wrong—I know it!"

There was an anxiety in his voice which communicated itself to Murrah and he walked over and rapped on the door.

"Open up thar!" he ordered roughly.

"In a minute!" answered a voice. Then the door swung open and Enright, the cattle-buyer, marched out. He was followed by three men who were indubitably gun-fighters; and in the lead, his eyes burning with the lust of battle, strode Gun-smoke, a gun on each hip.

"Just start something, you ugly man's dog!" he taunted; and Murrah stepped back with an oath. But he did not go for his gun.

"What's all this?" he demanded truculently.

"Never mind!" retorted Gun-smoke. "You think you're so bad—draw that gun and see where you light!"

"Who made any cracks about drawing a gun?" snarled

ZIM PLUNKETT MEETS HIS NEMESIS

Murrah, backing off. "We came hyer, by grab, for our money."

"Here it is," spoke up Enright cheerfully. And he drew a small roll from his pocket. "Just count that over," he said.

Quick looked at it and glanced at Scorp, whose close mouth was working in spasms.

"Is that all?" gasped Plunkett at last.

"That's all," replied Enright, "except these little mementoes that you left behind you in Texas."

He opened up a black hand-bag and as he spread out a pile of notes Plunkett's eyes bulged out of his head.

"Them's no good!" he snapped, cursing viciously.

"I beg leave to differ with you there," returned Enright. "I've hired some right smart lawyers and they tell me these notes are good—if presented in the state of Texas."

"W'y, the son-of-a-goat!" wailed Plunkett in despair. "I knowed he was up to some trick!" But Murrah had regained his nerve.

"Lemme look at them papers," he spoke up sharply, and Enright laid them out on the table.

"There's notes," he explained, "for four hundred and twenty thousand dollars, that Zimiriah Plunkett gave in Texas. I bought them up from the original holders and they're every one legal and good. But besides that there's the interest at ten per cent a year, running three years more or less—a total of a hundred and twenty-six thousand dollars, making five hundred and forty-six thousand, all told. Taking that from the price of these cattle makes twenty-three thousand, five hundred and thirty-six dollars, still due."

GUN-SMOKE

He laid down the roll of bills and Quick shuffled them over mechanically, glancing about the room as he worked. Over twenty men, all armed with six-shooters, stood frozen, waiting to shoot.

"O.K.," he pronounced, passing the roll to Plunkett. "Come on." And he started for the door.

"Don't forget these notes!" spoke up Enright pleasantly, and Old Scorp gave him a look.

"To hell with 'em!" he flung back angrily. "I'll take this out of yore hide!"

CHAPTER XVII

THE QUEEN OF THE BALL

THERE was blood on the moon when Zim Plunkett crossed the line and summoned his warriors to battle, but as he lined them up two men rode into town and dismounted in front of the bank. They wore no uniform, no badge and no star, but every man knew they were Rangers. And to kill a Texas Ranger was the Western equivalent of blowing out the gas. Also Quick Murrah, for once, was not drunk.

"I don't know, Dad," he said doubtfully as Scorp Plunkett came riding by. "Looks like we're being capped into a brace game. Because shore as hell if we charge across that street them Rangers will shoot *you* and *me*. They've got us spotted, right now."

"They's haf a million dollars right thar in that bank!" raved Scorp. "Ain't you got the nerve to go git it?"

"I doubt that like hell!" responded Murrah. "I don't believe we'll find a dollar. But one thing I do know—if I cross that line one or the other of them Rangers will kill me. They ain't forgot that tiger."

"W'y you cowardly son-of-a-goat!" cursed Plunkett. "You're scairt, by grab, of that Gun-smoke. Why didn't you draw yore gun when he p'intedly dared you? I thought yore front name was Quick?"

"Never mind about my name," grumbled Murrah. "I ain't no chuckleheaded fool. When I see I'm up ag'inst it, with gunmen all around me, I've got sense enough to quit the game. But jest because I quit don't you never think I'm licked. I'm only letting go to git a better holt—I'll fix that blow-hard yet!"

"Yes, you will!" sneered Plunkett, but though he railed and threatened he did not order the charge. He was out of his head with rage over the loss of his fortune but at the same time he was not courting sure death. The bank was built of stone, it housed thirty armed men and its vaults more than likely were empty. And if he killed a Texas Ranger neither distance nor time would save him from the Rangers' revenge. They would follow him to the ends of the world.

"Let 'em go!" he said at last, "let 'em laugh at their dirty trick. We'll sift back across the line when the Rangers ain't looking and collect Mr. Enright's hair."

He led the way into a saloon where for the first time in years he sought to drown his sorrows in drink; and the next day, haggard and broken, he rode back towards Portales, swaying and mumbling and cursing his luck. But when he recovered Zim Plunkett turned wolf. For three years he had stolen as the fox and weasel steal, by stealth and under cover of night. Now he came out in the open with his wolf-pack behind him and killed for the sheer love of killing. And after he had killed he robbed.

Once more the pushing settlers felt the weight of his

THE QUEEN OF THE BALL

heavy hand as he reached out to crush them down. Houses were burned, horses stolen, men killed in their homes, yet still the tide of people pressed on. It was a movement as resistless as the onthrust of a glacier, but Plunkett fought against it blindly. Yet as the summer wore on and they organized against him he learned to let the homesteaders alone.

At first secretly and then openly Dandy McAllister had welcomed the settlers and located them on land near his own. Then as the railroad took up its slow western march he threw open his grant to settlement. Land was leased for almost nothing or let out on shares, broad acres were put to the plow; and when Plunkett, riding south, beheld the houses along the creek-beds he could see the beginning of the end. For three years and more with his lawless Texas gunmen he had ruled the timid Mexicans like a king; the sheriff and his deputies had fled; but these men who came now were a different breed of citizens—they would fight in defense of their homes.

Midsummer had come and the rush was at its height, Zim Plunkett had retired to Portales; and the broad floor of the Casa Grande was scraped and waxed for a dance, to celebrate the founding of Barcee. No longer was it a mud settlement, a double row of houses where Mexicans sat basking in the sun; the Americans had come and the townsite was all laid out—with the railroad it would spring into life. But not for that alone did Dandy clear his hall and invite one and all to the dance. The Stone-eater and his daughter were almost forgotten, and Johnsie was to lead the grand march.

GUN-SMOKE

She came riding with her mother to the Casa Grande, to preside for one night as its Queen, for of all the settlers the Bloods had been the first to stick and defy Zim Plunkett. But Johnsie was queen also by virtue of her beauty; and the voluptuous Lolita had been relegated to the background, lest their feud break out anew. For this was a settlers' dance, not a Mexican *baile,* and Dandy had a question to ask. It was the same question, of course, which he had asked before, but this time he expected a different answer.

He received her with a deference which almost turned Johnsie's head, as if indeed she were a queen; and the Mexican servant-maids veiled their faces with black *rebozas,* the better to hide their stares. Yet as she stood in the great house whose mistress she might be Johnsie's eyes searched the shadows for the woman she hated and the doorways for the man she loved. But Lolita was well hid and over a year had passed since Gun-smoke had gone away. Then how could she think that he loved her?

She had heard of that bold stroke by which their outlawed notes had deprived Zim Plunkett of a fortune. She had heard of Gun-smoke, striding out from behind his father to dare Quick Murrah to draw. But Quick had not drawn; and Gun-smoke, alas, had not come to claim his horse. For now, if he came, she would have to give him Star-dust—that is, if she told Dandy: "Yes." But was Gun-smoke afraid, after all? Was he afraid to come back for the kiss? Or was he, even then, riding in across the plains to challenge Scorp Plunkett's power? She glanced about again for his big, yellow head, towering up above the crowd, and then the grand march began.

THE QUEEN OF THE BALL

Many girls were there now, some pretty, some plain, and each one had her swain; but as Johnsie, gracefully gowned, took her place at their head she was easily the prettiest of all. Dandy McAllister escorted her, wearing his heart on his sleeve; and as Johnsie glanced up at him she wondered if, after all, she was making a great mistake. He was so tall, so slim and handsome with his curly brown hair and his eyes always sparkling with fun; and the Big House, the Casa Grande, was so like a Southern mansion, only with Mexicans instead of slaves. Why not become the mistress of it all?

They danced and the music made her forget her fixed purpose, which was always to keep Dandy in his place. Among the crude, homespun settlers he seemed all the more the gentleman, the more fitted to preside over her home. They had responded at last to the spell of Mexican music with its nuances and syncopated time, and as the floor filled up Dandy whisked her into the patio, where there was nothing but flowers, and the stars. Johnsie wondered what strange destiny was shaping her life at that moment, and what her answer would be; but as she stood, half-resisting the tug at her hand, a pistol-shot came through the night.

"What's that?" she exclaimed, drawing back.

"Some drunk Mexican," he answered impatiently. "But say now, Johnsie, listen!"

Five shots rang out in rapid succession, there was a long-drawn-out wolf-like yell, and Dandy cursed under his breath.

"It's those Texans!" he muttered. "Damn!"

"Oh, will they come over here?" she gasped.

"No, no!" he assured her. "Just shooting up Mexicantown. My Lord, will you listen to that?"

A whole battery of pistols was being emptied at once, there was a wolf-howl that rent the air, and as Johnsie turned back towards the safety of the house the doorways gave up men.

"What's that? What's that shooting?" they all asked at once but Dandy did not reply.

"Come on!" he cried impulsively. "Let's go in and dance!" And Johnsie stepped in out of the night.

"Go ahead—what's the matter with you?" shouted McAllister to the orchestra which was beginning to falter and break time; and with Johnsie in his arms he whirled into a waltz; but the joy had suddenly gone out of it. From across the bridge the popping of pistols grew louder, there were loud whoops and drunken fusillades; and then above the music, which had sunk to a thin fiddling, there came the menacing thunder of rushing horses.

"My God!" wailed Dandy, "they're coming to break up the dance. That's Quick Murrah and those scoundrels from Portales—this is something they never did before!"

He turned irresolutely towards his weapons on the wall, then shook his head and looked back. Already the clatter of hoofs had entered the plaza and the settler men came swarming back.

"It's all right, folks!" announced McAllister. "Choose your partners for a waltz—and you fiddlers, go ahead and play!"

He scowled so threateningly that the orchestra struck up

THE QUEEN OF THE BALL

again, though nobody but Dandy danced; and then with a braggart clacking of highheeled boots Quick Murrah appeared in the door. On his legs were the tawny red and black shaps, made from the skin of the Bengal tiger; and for a vest he wore a garment of the same gorgeous hide, with two gun butts protruding below the flaps. He was smiling, but not at McAllister. It was Johnsie who held his gaze.

"Jest in time!" he said, bowing mockingly; and Johnsie saw he was drunk. His eyes had a fixed and glassy stare, he swayed slightly and his manner was insolent—but he was not too drunk to shoot.

"What do you want?" demanded Dandy as the settlers gazed in awe at this man-killing boss of the Night Riders. "Are you trying to break up our dance?"

"Hell—no!" answered Murrah with a drunken bow to the ladies. "I come to dance myse'f—with the Queen."

He leered significantly at the pale-faced Johnsie, and she turned instinctively to Dandy. But Dandy did not rise to the occasion.

"No, indeed!" disclaimed Murrah, advancing across the floor as his satellites crowded in from behind, "all I want is a dance—with the Queen." And he bowed once more to Johnsie.

"My dances are all taken," she answered tartly as Dandy stood tongue-tied and irresolute; and Murrah cocked his head at the crowd.

"Who's the gentleman," he demanded, "that's got the next dance? Step out, now—don't be bashful!" But no one claimed the honor.

"Some mistake," he observed, smiling confidently. "Come on, Johnsie, give me that dance."

"No!" she cried as her temper got the best of her, "I won't dance with you, Quick Murrah! Mr. McAllister, will you take me to my mother?"

"No, he won't," Murrah informed her insolently; and after a glance at his uninvited guest Dandy shrugged his shoulders and declined. For Quick Murrah would have to be indulged or the bullets would begin to fly.

"Now!" ordered Murrah, thrusting one elbow out towards Johnsie, "will you give me the honor and pleasure?"

He smiled ingratiatingly and for a moment, out of spite, Johnsie was tempted to accept his arm, then she turned with blazing eyes on Dandy.

"Mr. McAllister," she said, "are you a man or a mouse? He's drunk—will you allow him to insult me?"

"Oh—you're insulted, eh?" came back Murrah, after a menacing glance at Dandy, and his voice held a venomous calm. "So you think you're too good fer me, hey? Old Heck Blood's daughter—too good for Quick Murrah!" He laughed and glanced back at his men.

"It's too bad!" he mocked, thrusting his jaw out drunkenly and leering into her face. "It's too damned bad about you. Whar'd you git that pretty dress that you're wearing? Heh! It's charged up at Dandy's store!'

He put such a wealth of insinuation into his voice that Johnsie felt a blush of shame, but Dandy did not stir.

"Too good, eh?" Murrah sneered. "Whar'd you git that pinto pony you been riding hither and yon? You folks remember that hawse-thief—Gun-smoke? He stayed in her house—a month!"

"You lie!" cried Johnsie, out of her head with rage. Then, driven to madness by his mocking smile, she leapt forward and slapped him, hard.

"Shut your mouth!" she commanded. "Shut your mouth and leave this hall, you ignorant, drunken fool! If my father was heah, he'd kill you!"

"He would not!" swaggered Murrah, "Heck Blood or any other man! And I come fer that dance—understand?"

He held out his elbow and Johnsie glanced at Dandy, then turned and walked regally away.

"You won't get it," she stated. "And Dandy McAllister —you're a coward!"

She flung a look over her shoulder that made Dandy blench and hurried across the room to her mother.

"You're a coward!" she called back. "And Quick Murrah, you're a coward! The next time I see you, I'll kill you!"

"Go ahead and shoot!" laughed Murrah. "You know I'll die happy, Johnsie. But don't you never think I won't git what I come fer—and by grab you'll pay for that slap!"

Johnsie stood in the doorway gazing back at them hatefully—at the man who had insulted her and the man who, in the pinch, had feared to protect her good name. Then she flung up her hand dismissing them both, and rushed out into the night.

CHAPTER XVIII

Quick Murrah Eats Dirt

THE SETTLERS' BALL at Barcee broke up in confusion with Quick Murrah, hand on hip, swaggering forth unhindered to vent his spite on the town. Every house in Barcee had its broken window or bullet-hole to pay for the slap at his pride and then, drunker than ever, he returned to the Big House and put on a show in the square. Horses wheeled in flying squadrons, pistol-shots stabbed the night and awakened the echoes of the fort, but the stout heart of Morgan McAllister had ceased to beat and his son lacked the nerve of his sire. He kept cover and the Texans rode away.

The story of Murrah's sneers lost nothing in the telling and Johnsie, humiliated, hid her head in the lonely cabin, for no knight had come to her aid. A hundred settlers, and Dandy McAllister, had stood supine while Quick Murrah insulted her, but her anger flamed up most against Dandy. He was her partner for the dance, he was the owner of the house, but neither by word nor deed had he attempted to defend her—and yet how often had he protested his love! Johnsie wept with helpless rage, and then one morning at dawn she saw Gun-smoke riding up to the gate.

He had a rifle beneath his knee, two pistols hung in his

QUICK MURRAH EATS DIRT

belt; and as Watch-eye came to the bars he cleared them at a bound and gave forth a high, ringing neigh. An answering call from up the canyon made him fight against the bit; and as Star-dust appeared galloping furiously to meet him, they touched noses and whickered with delight. But though she had seen them come Johnsie turned back and shut the door and Gun-smoke gazed about him dubiously.

A year had passed since he had ridden away from Blood's Canyon and found Johnsie waiting at the bars, a year without a word of good or ill. Times had changed—but he had ridden far.

"Hello, the house!" he hailed and as the hounds set up their baying Heck Blood came stumbling to the door. Gun-smoke stared, for the Colonel was drunk.

"Well, who are you?" he demanded intolerantly. "Who are you—and what's your business?"

"I'm Enright—Bill Enright," announced Gun-smoke quietly; and the Colonel rubbed his bleared eyes.

"You're a liar!" he exclaimed abusively. "You're that hawse-thief, Gun-smoke, that I warned away from my do'!"

"No, Colonel," responded Gun-smoke patiently, "you never warned me away, at all. How's Mrs. Blood—and Johnsie?"

The Colonel stepped out the door and closed it behind him, then strode out threateningly towards Gun-smoke.

"You worthless whelp!" he quavered, "what the devil do you mean, sending hawses and presents to my daughter? I've a damned good mind to kill you—haven't you heard what people are saying? They say you made those presents for a purpose!"

"A purpose!" repeated Gun-smoke blankly and the Colonel burst out cursing.

"Yes, a purpose!" he raged, "and a low-down, scoundrelly purpose—taking advantage, suh, of her innocence, and a young girl's love of pleasure, to attempt to lead her astray!"

"Who says that?" demanded Gun-smoke thickly.

"Who says it?" repeated the Colonel, swaying drunkenly. "Quick Murrah, the renegade, he says it! He made those charges, suh, at a public hall, and not one dared to deny them. And now my wife and daughter won't let me leave the canyon. Because if I try to punish Quick, he'll kill me. But a man's honor, suh—isn't that worth dying for? And the honor and good name of his daughter? I'm slow now, I admit it, and Quick Murrah can out-shoot me——"

"You leave him to me!" broke in Gun-smoke wrathfully. "I'll tame him, the cowardly whelp. And if he don't come back and apologize to Johnsie——" He choked and reined his horse towards the gate.

"You kill him!" shouted the Colonel; and Gun-smoke nodded.

He rowelled the reluctant Watch-eye, who was fighting his head to stay with Star-dust, until he squealed and took the gate at a bound; and then in a cloud of dust he galloped off up the trail towards Portales and the man he sought. The huge log which blocked the road was nothing to him now, nor to panting, sweat-lathered Watch-eye; and as they landed before the doorway of the ZIP saloon Gun-smoke swung down and strode inside.

Groups of outlaws sat in poker games that had endured since the night before, others slept in their blankets on the

QUICK MURRAH EATS DIRT

floor; but Quick Murrah and his brothers were standing before the bar and they turned as the stranger approached.

"Out of the way, there!" ordered Gun-smoke, motioning the brothers aside, "Quick Murrah is the man I'm after! But if you want to chip in I'll take you on, too. Now, Bad Man, pull your gun!"

He slapped his holster significantly and held his right hand poised, but Murrah did not go for his guns. He was startled, and his nerves were slack.

"What's the matter?" he demanded. "What's biting ye?"

"Never mind!" cursed Gun-smoke. "Draw your gun and shoot it out. All three of ye—I don't give a dam'! The man don't live that can say what you did, about Johnsie Blood and that horse!"

"What hawse?" challenged Murrah, snatching at any straw to stave off the impending fight. "What hawse? I never said nothing."

"Yes you did!" charged Gun-smoke. "You said I gave Johnsie that horse to—to take advantage of her, like! Now damn you, shoot or eat dirt!"

He slapped his holster again and out the door behind him the Night Riders scuttled like rats. But the bullets did not come.

"Oh, that?" nodded Murrah. "I was drunk."

"Yes, and you're drunk yet, you son-of-a-goat!" stormed Gun-smoke. "Draw your gun—any of you—all of you! I've come here to kill you but I'll even give a snake a chance. You'll shoot or come back and apologize!"

"I'll apologize, then," agreed Quick Murrah promptly. "By grab, I never meant nothin'! W'y, sure I'll apologize;

GUN-SMOKE

because I know damned well every word that I said was a lie."

"And won't you fight at all?" wailed Gun-smoke.

"No!" laughed Quick. "Why the hell should *we* fight?" And while Gun-smoke watched him hopefully Murrah saddled his fastest horse and rode off down the trail to Blood's Canyon.

The Colonel slammed the door when he saw Quick's well-remembered horse, and Watch-eye following behind; but Murrah's belt of pistols was slung over Gun-smoke's saddle-horn and the killer rode up meekly to the door. He was tamed, but there was death in his eye.

"Colonel Blood," he began, "I've come down to apologize for what I said at the dance about Johnsie. I was drunk, and every word was a lie."

"Git down," ordered Gun-smoke as Johnsie came out. "Git down on your knees, and say it. Now, you foul-mouthed whelp, I'm going to give you back these guns and I hope to Gawd you'll draw."

He threw down the belt of guns but Murrah shook his head.

"I don't care for 'em," he said. "You can keep 'em."

"I don't want 'em!" yelled Gun-smoke. "Put 'em on and fight, you yap!" But Murrah backed off towards his horse.

"You wouldn't shoot a man in cold blood, would you?" he whimpered; and Gun-smoke gave up in disgust.

"No!" he replied, "but you ain't a man, so don't you tempt me too far. Now git, you ugly man's dog!"

He jerked his head down the canyon and Quick Murrah swung up and turned his horse away.

QUICK MURRAH EATS DIRT

"That's all right," he said. "See you again, Mr. Gun-smoke." And with a quick, appeasing smile he was gone.

"Why the devil," stormed the Colonel, "didn't you kill the dirty whelp? Now he'll come back and shoot you from ambush?"

"Well," retorted Gun-smoke, "you had a gun right there. Why didn't *you* shoot him, Colonel Blood?"

"I'm not in the habit, suh," returned the Colonel with drunken dignity, "of shooting down unarmed men. But what's to prevent him from denying this apology, the low-flung, unprincipled hound?"

"There's his gun-belt," suggested the practical Gun-smoke. "Just drape that across your piano and ask 'em how come it's there."

"What do you mean, suh?" flared up the Colonel. "Do you intend any reflections on my home, by that slighting reference to a piano? I'll give you to understand, suh, that while I'm poor, I'm proud! The Bloods were all gentlemen—all of them! But my daughter has no piano!"

"Now, Henry," interposed Mrs. Blood, "please don't start in to arguing. Mr. Gun-smoke has brought Quick down heah and forced him to apologize——"

"Yes, by gad!" broke in the Colonel, "but if he'd kept his cussed hawse no apologies, my dear woman, would be necessary. Evil words travel so fast that truth can never catch them, and a woman's fairest jewel is her good name. Mistuh Gun-smoke, suh, my daughter has small reason to thank you for the present of that ornery, spotted hawse!"

"Ornery!" yelped Gun-smoke, "why, you danged old walloper, that pinto is own brother to Watch-eye!"

GUN-SMOKE

"You take that hawse away!" commanded the Colonel wrathfully, "and don't you dare to bring him back. You've been a disturbing factor in my home, Mistuh Gun-smoke, bringing reflections on my daughter's good name."

"Oh, now, Henry!" pleaded Mrs. Blood tearfully. "You've been drinking—you don't know what you're saying."

"Madame!" thundered the Colonel, "I don't need you, nor anyone, to tell me how to safeguard my home! You take that pinto away, suh, and don't you come back heah. You—you're a disturbing factor, in my home."

"I'll do nothing of the kind," answered Gun-smoke defiantly. "That horse is your daughter's, and until she gives it back to me it stays right here—understand? She saved my life one time, when Quick Murrah wanted to hang me, and that's why I sent her the horse!"

"Oh, was it?" cried Johnsie, who had been listening in moody silence. "Then I *can* keep him; can't I, Mother?"

"You sure can!" responded Gun-smoke, "because I'm leaving here right now, and I won't be back very shortly. The man don't live, drunk or sober, that can warn me away from his home. Good day, Mrs. Blood. So long, Johnsie— the horse is yours. You can go plumb to hell, Colonel Blood, suh!"

He jerked his horse right about and sent him down the hill with a savage jab of the spurs; nor did he look back when Johnsie bounded after him, waving her hand in a last good-bye. He took the bars at a leap and galloped furiously towards Barcee, to drown his sorrows in the flowing bowl.

CHAPTER XIX

The Duel

THE sight of a tall Texan, charging purposefully into town, sent the Barcee Mexicans scuttling; but when Gun-smoke stepped down and entered the *cantina* they came out again, for they knew his horse. Here was the yellow-haired Texano who had driven Queek Murrah from town, to win a kiss from Lolita. He was the man who in this same saloon had dared the Murrah brothers to fight; and who, at four hundred yards, had shot the shirt from Queek's back, making a groove in the flesh above his heart. *Que diablo*—if only it had killed him!

Gun-smoke ordered a drink and the beans and tortillas, but as he sat at the lunch-counter making up for his long fast he was aware of a face that he knew. It was Juan Brabon, the Stone-eater.

"*Kai, Come-piedras!*" he greeted; and the Stone-eater advanced, hat in hand.

"Have a drink!" invited Gun-smoke, but Juan declined deferentially and presented a scribbled note.

"From El Patron!" he said and stood waiting.

Gun-smoke spread out the paper and read it over thoughtfully. It was from McAllister, asking him to see him at once. But Gun-smoke felt no yearning for company.

"Tell the patron I am busy," he ordered.

"Ah, sí—sí señor!" responded the Stone-eater obsequiously. "But the gentleman will come soon, no?"

"Nope," grumbled Gun-smoke, "I'm going to git drunk and I don't need no outside help."

"Muy bien," replied Brabon after a minute of dazed silence and bowed himself out the door. But Dandy was not accustomed to take "No" for an answer and as Gun-smoke prepared to embark on his *solamente* El Patron came hurrying through the door.

"What's all this?" he demanded as he saw the large black bottle. "What's the matter with you—got a grouch?"

"Yes!" answered Gun-smoke after a moment of brooding silence; and Dandy sat down beside him.

"So've I?" he declared sympathetically. "Did you hear about it?"

"About what?" enquired Gun-smoke ungraciously.

"Why, about Quick Murrah breaking up our Settlers' Ball and—and getting nasty to Johnsie!"

"I done paid him for that," stated Gun-smoke. "Rode plumb up there this morning and made him get down on his knees and admit he was a dadburned liar. Took his guns away, and everything—the poor yap was afraid to fight."

"You did!" exclaimed Dandy. "This morning? Well, you saved me the battle of my life. Because after what Johnsie said there was nothing for me to do but kill him, or die in the attempt."

"Yeah?" observed Gun-smoke sarcastically. "Well, just what did Johnsie say?"

"Never mind," sighed McAllister, flagging the barkeep

THE DUEL

for a glass and pouring out a drink from the bottle. "Well, that's all over, anyway. Here's to you!"

He tossed off the whisky and Gun-smoke eyed him glumly as he poured another libation to the gods.

"Didn't hear about your trouble," he said at last. "The Colonel gimme hell for sending that horse to Johnsie—said I was a disturbing influence in his home! So I just told the old sot—he was drunker than a goat—to go where the wicked soldier went. The man don't live that can talk to me like *that!* And after I'd brought Quick clean down there, to boot!"

"What! Did you bring him clear down from Portales?" exclaimed Dandy incredulously. "And make him apologize to Johnsie?"

"To Johnsie and everybody—and admit he was a low-down liar! But do you think that bought me anything? Ump-umm, the old Colonel insulted me!"

"He's been drinking," confided Dandy, "don't mind him. But, Gun-smoke, you just got back here in time, because Quick Murrah has been raising *hell*. He's been rank enough, Gawd knows; but ever since Old Scorp lost those cattle on his notes the whole outfit has been on the prod. They're gathering their cattle, too, inside that big pasture; and between you and me I believe they're planning a clean-up, and then a quick get-away north."

"They're whipped, then," nodded Gun-smoke. "It's got too hot for 'em."

"Absolutely—not!" denied Dandy. "We're whipped, but I've got through crawling. From now on I'm going to hire every gunman that comes through here, and fight the devil with fire. That's why I sent word to come over."

GUN-SMOKE

"Nothing doing!" returned Gun-smoke as he caught his meaning. "You can't take *me* on as no gunman. I'm going to leave this cussed country."

"But why?" pleaded McAllister. "We need you!"

"Maybe *you* do," conceded Gun-smoke, "but the rest of 'em—ump-umm! I don't even draw a pleasant look!"

"I know!" laughed Dandy, leaning back and slapping his leg. "You've had another quarrel with Johnsie! But don't get mad, Old Man; I was just about to say I've had a quarrel, myself. But come on, Pardner, there's no hard feeling—come over to the house where we can get some real whisky and we'll drink to her lovely, black eyes."

"I'll go—for the whisky," decided Gun-smoke at last; and rose up wearily from his seat. It was a slow, heartbreaking business, getting drunk.

In the cool living-room of the Big House, with Watch-eye out in the corral looking back up the trail for Stardust, the dreary round of drinks went on; and meanwhile as through a haze Gun-smoke heard Dandy talking and saw women moving to and fro. One smiled at him radiantly, but his face did not change—it was Lolita, and he was thinking of Johnsie. Night came, and swift oblivion; then dawn with its keen, cold air and a man's voice clamoring at his door.

"What you want?" he demanded at last.

"Here's a letter for you!" answered Dandy. "Found it lying on the floor. It came from Quick Murrah," he added.

"The ornery scrub!" grumbled Gun-smoke as he reared up and took in the note. "What the devil does he want, now?"

He read the letter over hastily, then hurled it contemptuously on the floor.

THE DUEL

"It's a challenge," he laughed, "and look at my hand! Couldn't do much shooting with *that*. Ump-umm—it trembles too much. You tell the danged whelp he had his chance yesterday." And he laid down and went to sleep.

Quick Murrah had had his chance, and he had feared to draw and shoot, even at Portales with his men all around him; but now he sent challenge after insulting challenge, and at last Gun-smoke rose up and dressed.

"You tell him," he roared, "that I'll fight when I'm good and ready. Tell him to come in and git me, if he can't keep his shirt on. Tell him I don't give a dam'—he can wait."

"But this Mexican boy," protested Dandy, "says he's terrorizing the town! He's cleaned out one cantina, already!"

"Well, *you* go and tame him," answered back Gun-smoke morosely. "Seems like every time I come here you try to cap me into some fight."

"It's none of my doings!" denied McAllister heatedly. "He showed up at daylight, rode his horse into that end saloon and he's been sending out challenges ever since."

"Yes, and it's a thousand to one he's got both his brothers with him, or planted where they can shoot me on sight. What does he think I am, a danged fool?"

Gun-smoke grumbled to himself as he ate a hearty breakfast and steadied his nerves with coffee; then, strapping on his guns, he went out to the corral and heaved the saddle up on Watch-eye.

"This is a hell of a country," he said, tightening his cinch up viciously; and Watch-eye snapped his teeth like castanets. "Yes, and now *you* want a fight!" he complained, stepping back. "But you bite me, Mistuh Hawse, and you'll regret

GUN-SMOKE

it." He pulled the latigo up ruthlessly and Watch-eye laid back his ears, while Gun-smoke gave a hectoring laugh. But when the saddle was firmly cinched he began to fumble through his pockets and Watch-eye was suddenly appeased.

"I wonder," observed Gun-smoke, "what I did with all that *sugar*!" And at the word Watch-eye whickered and drew closer. "Nope," he teased, "it ain't here—and it ain't *here*. Well, you don't need to bunt me over. I had it for you, all the time!" And he fetched three cubes of sugar from his pocket.

"Now!" he began, when the pinto had mumbled them up and crunched them between his strong teeth, "they've got us in a jack-pot, Watch-eye. Got to fight or run away, and I don't want to do either. Shall we go in and clean up on that Quick?"

Watch-eye stood at attention, his glassy eyes staring, and Gun-smoke scratched his towsled head dubiously.

"Want to go back to Texas?" he enquired. "Oh, hell; let's go out and see the town!"

He swung up into the saddle and trotted out of the plaza, but at the end of the bridge he stopped. The long street was deserted, but on tops of their flat houses he could see the Mexicans, crouching like jack-rabbits. The town was under bombardment.

"We done wrong, Bronk," said Gun-smoke as he heard a pistol popping and saw women rushing out of a house, "we shore made one grand mistake when we left our happy home to come to a deadfall like this. But Texas expects every man to do his duty."

He drew out his pistols and filled the hammer chambers,

THE DUEL

giving him a full six shots for each gun; and as he sat his horse in silence Dandy McAllister slipped out and looked up and down the street.

"Kinder spooky," observed Gun-smoke. "I don't like the looks of things. Ask Juan if Quick's brothers are in town."

"No," answered Dandy, "he says Quick came alone. He's up around that last cantina."

"So I see," replied Gun-smoke as some Mexicans came flying out. "Well, I've got through fooling with that fellow. You get me a rifle and I'll shoot from here—him and his brothers are laying to kill me."

McAllister ran in and brought out his rifle, and as Gun-smoke saw him bringing it, he smiled.

"It's a wonder," he said, "that a crack shot like you wouldn't pull this off himself. What's the matter—got a yaller streak, somewhere?"

"No! I'm not afraid!" snapped back Dandy, stung to the quick, "only——"

"Well, I'll tell you what you do, then," directed Gun-smoke. "You follow along behind me and watch these houses, and the top of that butte up yonder. I'm game to take on Quick—it's Ed and John I'm thinking of. If they try to ambush me, you shoot."

"Well—all right," agreed McAllister, heaving a sigh, "only——"

"For cripes' sake!" burst out Gun-smoke, "be a man, for once in your life! Will you do it, now? Yes or no?"

"I'll do it!" answered Dandy quietly.

"All right, then," said Gun-smoke, dismounting. "My Old Man would give me hell for taking a chance like this,

175

but I've got to play my hand out, now. If anything happens notify Enright and Valentine, the cattle-buyers. Come on, Watch-eye—they'd plug you, sure."

He led him back under cover of the thick adobe wall and dropped his reins on the ground. Then, hitching up his belt he started up the street with Dandy a hundred feet behind. At the corner of the first house he stopped and looked ahead, but the broad street was empty and deserted.

"Come out and fight!" he yelled, shooting his gun into the air; but Murrah kept cover—he was waiting.

"The murdering whelp!" cursed Gun-smoke, "he's hiding to shoot me somewhere." And with a quick burst of speed he ran forward to the next building, holding his guns in each hand as he charged.

"Come out and fight!" he hollered again; and from the saloon far up the street Quick Murrah stepped out, reeling. He was attired in the full regalia of a border warrior, with his tiger-skin shaps and vest, and he carried a gun in each hand.

"He's drunk!" called Gun-smoke in disgust; but Dandy motioned him on. His eyes were burning now, his lips were set tight—Gun-smoke could see he was on tiptoes to kill.

"Whee! Yeee-pah!" yelled Murrah, shooting off both guns at once; and Gun-smoke stepped out, crouching.

A bullet whizzed past his ear and, though the distance was far, he threw down and fired—once, twice. But now the maudlin Murrah was no longer drunk. He shot close and fast and Gun-smoke's hat was knocked off before he had walked ten feet. He ducked against the wall as a bullet grazed his ribs and then with a smash a great slug struck in

THE DUEL

front of him, throwing gravel in his face as it bounced. It had come from the side and like a flash Gun-smoke dodged and butted his way through a door. Two more slugs, like angry hornets, followed close on his heels; and then Dandy's rifle rang out.

"I got him!" he called and, running zig-zag to escape Quick's bullets, he rushed up and whisked in the door.

"He's up on that butte!" he panted, smashing a window to thrust out his gun; and for a long time they waited in silence. Then from far up the street they heard the clatter of horses' feet and Gun-smoke popped his head out to look. Quick Murrah was galloping off, his brother John followed close behind; and in the rear, dragged along by the neck, there ran a horse with an empty saddle.

"You killed Ed," observed Gun-smoke quietly and Dandy shrank back with a groan.

CHAPTER XX

An Indian Never Forgets

QUICK MURRAH had been drunk, but not as crazy drunk as his shooting and yelling had indicated. His attack on the town had been staged for a purpose, to lure Gun-smoke within range of his guns; but though he had reeled into the street the last bullet he fired had just missed Gun-smoke's heart. And that bullet had saved Gun-smoke's life, for as he whirled from the impact Ed Murrah had fired from the butte. Murrah had missed him by so much as his next step would have taken him—and at the smash of the slug Gun-smoke had ducked. Ed had shot again, twice; and, spotting the puffs of smoke, Dandy McAllister had laid him low.

It had all been over in the space of a few seconds, and then Dandy's tense nerves snapped. The whirligig of fate had flung Gun-smoke, the reckless fighter, unhurt into a waiting doorway; while McAllister, following behind to cover his rear, had fired the fatal shot.

"My God!" he exclaimed as he stared out the broken window at the sprawling form on the butte, "the whole gang will be down on us, now. I knew it all the time—I knew the first shot I fired those Murrahs would come and get me!"

AN INDIAN NEVER FORGETS

"Yes, but they haven't got you yet!" Gun-smoke reminded him scornfully. "You had to fight it out with them, sometime. Send out and get some gunmen and stand the rascals off. Come on, let's go up on the butte."

They slipped out the doorway and as no bullets smashed about them Gun-smoke led the way to the body. Murrah lay behind a rock, his rifle at his side, a bullet-hole between his narrow eyes. It had been a wonderful shot, one shot in a thousand, and as the Mexican villagers gathered about openmouthed, the Stone-eater re-inacted the deed. El Patron had suspected the well-known treachery of the Texanos; he had followed unobserved behind Gun-smoke; and as this Texan —he kicked him—had shot down into the street he had fired and killed him dead. Behold—with a bullet between the eyes!

Dandy gazed off up the road, where a trailing line of dust marked the flight of Quick Murrah towards Portales; but he could not but thrill to the praise of his peon, and when the Stone-eater had finished he spoke purposefully.

"Juan," he directed, "send messengers to the settlers and tell them to come to my house. I will hire all the fighting men for five dollars a day—the rest will be safe from Quick. This is only the beginning," he added, and Gun-smoke nodded grimly.

It was indeed the beginning of the end, the first blow in the final battle between the settlers and Zim Plunkett's rustlers, and he sent a messenger galloping to Texmex. Then as the settlers came swarming in, many bringing their wives and families and all of them armed for the fight, he sent another messenger to Heck Blood. All the cruel, vindictive rage of Quick Murrah and his riders had been unleashed by McAllister's chance shot; and the memory of his forced apology to Johnsie would rouse Quick to furious reprisals.

After breaking up the dance and humiliating McAllister he had been content to let Johnsie's words pass; but when, surprised by Gun-smoke, he had been compelled to retract his slurs, his anger had been fanned to a flame. At dawn, cursing and shooting, he had run amuck in Barcee, but once more his treacherous plans had failed and McAllister had shot down Ed. There would be no waiting now, no jockeying for position, for his half-Indian nature had been stirred to the depths—he was dangerous as a rabid wolf. That very night, in spite of Zim Plunkett, he would come riding to claim his revenge, and the Big House was turned into a fort.

The old loop-holes from which Morg McAllister and his vaqueros had fought off the swarming Comanches were opened up and guns were laid out. Scouts were posted on the roof and as the settlers came riding in Gun-smoke organized the fighting-men into a posse. In the store Dandy McAllister issued rifles and cartridges until the last of his peons was armed, for the time had come when he must fight or die and at least they could defend the fort.

All day in their covered wagons settlers had been hurrying in, though many refused to abandon their homes; but as evening approached and the Bloods did not arrive Gunsmoke hurried into the house to find Dandy.

"Where's the Colonel and his folks?" he demanded anxiously. "Didn't you send up a cowboy to get them?"

"Why, sure!" defended Dandy. "But the old man was drunk, I guess. Told the cowboy he wouldn't come down."

"But my Lord, Dandy!" protested Gun-smoke. "We can't leave them up there, alone. Think of Johnsie! And Mrs. Blood!"

"Well what are you going to do?" cried McAllister. "They refused to come in, the whole family. And then, to cap the climax, the Colonel's hounds took after a lion and he jumped on his horse and rode after them. So the cowboy turned around and came home."

"I'll go up there, myself," decided Gun-smoke.

"No you won't!" snapped back Dandy, "I need you. If you go, who'll take charge of that posse?"

"Well, you can," suggested Gun-smoke. "They all know you."

"Say, now listen!" clamored McAllister. "You got me into this, didn't you? Didn't you get me to shoot Ed Murrah? Well, do you think it's quite fair then, to go off and leave me, just when Quick and the Night Riders are due? What do they care about the Colonel, anyhow? I'm the man they're after, and you know it!"

"Well, sure," admitted Gun-smoke. "But you've got all these settlers——"

"That isn't enough!" broke in Dandy. "I want you here, to take charge of the posse. This is going to be a battle and——"

"Thar's a big fire, up at Portales!" shouted a voice from above, and Dandy and Gun-smoke made for the roof.

Dusk was falling on the wide plains, and in the deep canyons of the mountains, and far to the north a flame leapt and glowed against the black of the northern pass.

"They're whipped!" declared Gun-smoke. "They're burning their houses." But even as he spoke another blaze flared up, and this time it was out on the plain.

"Nope. They're burning the settlers' houses!" announced Dandy; but while they were arguing a third fire appeared and Gun-smoke knew the truth.

"Those are signal fires!" he said. "They're calling their men together. Well, boys, we're in for it. They mean business."

One by one the fires leapt up until in a long line they lapped down across the plains and touched the mountains against Barcee. Then, up on the high peak that overlooked the town, a new fire began to wink and glow. It was answered by a blaze from a point further north, mysterious signals were flashed to and fro. The fires burned down and black darkness came on, to cover up the deeds that were afoot.

In hushed groups the settlers gathered to watch for the flames that would announce the destruction of their homes, Gun-smoke's posse was saddled to ride; but as hour after hour brought nothing for all their waiting the settlers dispersed for the night. Midnight came and the very stars were obscured by a murk that spread out across the sky, and still Gun-smoke waited and watched. Then it came, a dull glow reflected on the clouds that hung above the gash of Blood's Canyon. It flickered and burned low and his heart leapt with hope, but the next minute it mounted to a flame.

"Get your horses!" yelled Gun-smoke. "Blood's house is afire!" And with his posse he ran to mount.

They rode helter-skelter through the long, deserted street;

AN INDIAN NEVER FORGETS

and once out in the open they saw a blaze of light like the reflection from a molten caldron. The high portals of the canyon obscured the fire itself but as well as he knew anything Gun-smoke knew that the Colonel's cabin was even then going up in flame. He rode hard up the long, long trail but the glow had died away before they came to the mouth of the canyon.

Watch-eye leapt over the bars of the well-remembered gate while Gun-smoke, cursing brokenly, spurred up towards the heap of embers that had once been Johnsie Blood's home. He had known he would be too late, but there by the ruins stood the Colonel.

"They're gone!" he shouted, waving his long arms into the vacancy of the night. "I've looked, but I can't find a sign of them. This is Quick Murrah's work, Mistuh Gun-smoke."

"Yes, of course it is!" raged Gun-smoke. "But why the hell didn't you come in when we sent out a cowboy from town? Did you hear any shooting, Colonel?"

"Not a shot," returned the Colonel solemnly. "My wife and daughter are prisoners."

"Well, by grab, we'll get 'em back, then!" answered Gun-smoke hotly. "Come on, boys—let's ride for Portales!"

The posse, stringing in, had lined up in front of the fire but as they wheeled to spur away the Colonel stopped them.

"Be careful, boys!" he warned. "For God's sake don't start to shooting. Because if Amy and Johnsie are theah——"

"All right, Colonel!" they called back and were off at a gallop. But to Gun-smoke, who led the way, there came a

GUN-SMOKE

voice louder than the Colonel's which bade him ride hard—and shoot. Johnsie had flouted Quick Murrah and slapped his swarthy face, and an Indian never forgets. Dandy McAllister that very day had shot down Murrah's brother, and an Indian never forgets. Gun-smoke had ridden far to take the part of this woman—he had made Quick Murrah eat dirt—and an Indian never forgets. Gun-smoke cursed as he rode, and whipped the faithful Watch-eye for Murrah had stolen women before.

CHAPTER XXI

Divided Counsel

IT was dawn when the flagging posse came in sight of Portales, its stone houses half blocking the narrow gateway that lay between the high, rocky walls. But nothing moved—even the dogs had disappeared—and on the wind there came the bellowing of cattle and the shrill, distant yells of cowboys.

"They've gone!" exclaimed Gun-smoke, wiping the sweat from his eyes and gazing far up among the pines; and there in a long line, like the writhing body of a snake, he could see the great herd inching on. So slowly did it move that only here and there a spot of red and white shifted by; but the posse set up a shout, for at last Zim Plunkett had been dislodged from his robbers' stronghold.

The greatest band of rustlers ever organized in the West was giving up its losing fight; they were moving over the Culebras into the wilds of Colorado, to carry on their depredations there; but, though they went, they drove thousands of stolen cattle before them and their warriors still guarded the pass. As the posse bunched up, just out of range from the gate, there was a puff of white smoke from Zim Plunkett's big house and a bullet came winging past. Then as if at a signal twenty guns belched at once and the posse broke for shelter in the wash.

GUN-SMOKE

Creeping up behind the cut-bank where the creek, winding down, had sluiced out its way across the plain, Gun-smoke gazed across the flat at the huddle of stone houses where Plunkett was making his last stand. They were loop-holed now and at every shot from the posse a dozen big guns spoke at once; but it was not to seize their cattle that Gun-smoke had come—he had no thought now except for Johnsie. For if, behind those walls, she and her mother were held prisoner, they must strike quickly and cut off a retreat. But if on the other hand Quick Murrah had hurried on, leaving the Riders to defend the pass, then they must circle and take up his trail. Gun-smoke crept up the creek-bed, closer and closer at every turn, until at last he caught a flutter of white. Then out of the big house Quick Murrah stepped boldly forth, and behind him there came a woman—it was Johnsie.

Not a gun was fired now as Murrah, at his ease, stood gazing out across the flat. He held up a square of paper with an insolent gesture and, as Mrs. Blood appeared beside him, he placed it in her hand.

"He's sending out a letter, boys!" called back Gun-smoke and ran up a white handkerchief on a stick. His heart was hammering now, for Johnsie was looking out wistfully—but she was safe, and the rest could wait. All night as he rode a great fear had pressed upon him until it left him sick and faint, but now he saw that Quick Murrah had seized her to protect the Night Riders' retreat. She was his hostage, and Murrah was still sane.

All night he had had the picture of a swarthy brute turned madman, and of Johnsie and her mother hurried off over the mountains to some hold-out hidden away in the hills. He

DIVIDED COUNSEL

had pictured the leering triumph of this scoundrel she had rebuffed as he held her at last in his power, but now like a bad dream the fears passed away and he beheld only Quick Murrah, the cow-thief. It was to protect the slow herds, the gatherings of years of stealing, that Johnsie had been carried away; and in spite of his rage over the death of his brother, Quick Murrah still obeyed Old Scorp. They were jockeying for time, to save their cattle.

Mrs. Blood came hurrying with the message in her hand and at sight of Gun-smoke looking up over the bank she cried out and broke into a run.

"Oh, they've kept her!" she sobbed as she stumbled down the bank; but Gun-smoke only snatched at the note.

Keep away you yaller-bellied smart ellick. I've got you wher I want you. You leav us alone or Ile take her over the mountains. Yule never see her again. I mean bizness—and then Ile kill her. Keep away and Ile turn her loose. Quick Murrah.

"He's a dadburned liar!" cursed Gun-smoke; but Mrs. Blood clutched at him, trembling.

"It's her only chance!' she pleaded. "Oh, please, please don't do anything! I'm afraid—I'm afraid of Quick!"

"I should have killed him!" grumbled Gun-smoke. "And I had him under my guns, three times. But he's a snake, Mrs. Blood. You can't trust him. I'm going to surround that house!"

"No! If you do, they'll kill her!" she protested. "I know them—and Quick is drunk."

"He's always drunk!" spat Gun-smoke vindictively. "But —well, I'll leave it to the boys."

GUN-SMOKE

He crept back down the wash to where the posse had assembled in a big open circle of sand, but as they argued back and forth another posse came riding in and took shelter behind the bank. It was Dandy McAllister and the sheriff of the county, who had returned to take part in the fight. And with them came the Colonel, sober at last. His cold eyes were burning now with a rage that only killing could quench; but after listening to his wife, who clung to him hysterically, the Colonel shook his head.

"No, gentlemen," he said, "I don't want a gun fired until my daughter has been returned by Quick Murrah. He's drunk, and in a murderous mood. He told my wife repeatedly that he'd shoot Johnsie down the moment we began an attack."

"Let's surround them!" suggested the sheriff, "and cut them off from Horse-thief Pass. Before night I'll have a hundred more men on the ground—and every one of you gentlemen is deputized. This is a struggle for law and order after years of open violence and I don't propose to let Plunkett escape."

He shook his head vigorously and many settlers applauded him, but Dandy McAllister was against him.

"No!" he objected. "Mr. Hanna may be our sheriff, but I for one refuse to be deputized. We may have to go against his orders. In a case like this with Johnsie's life at stake, her father and mother should decide. Now how do you feel about it, Colonel?"

"Gentlemen," began the Colonel, "we're at the mercy of a band of cut-throats, the most desperate gang of rustlers in the West. They're driving off their cattle and until that

DIVIDED COUNSEL

drive is finished they'll dare anything, do anything, to gain time. Quick Murrah is a man that I'd never trust a minute, because I know he's got Indian blood. All those sentiments of chivalry and of respect for a good woman which you will find in the lowest white have been left out of his cowardly carcass; but Zim Plunkett is the boss, and if we agree to spare his cattle I believe he'll have Johnsie sent back."

"Yes, and suppose he doesn't!" demanded the sheriff. "What then? Now we've got him in our power, and within the borders of our county; but over those mountains he'll be in Colorado, and in a wild, rocky country, to boot. But let me send a posse of men to cut them off from Horse-thief Pass and I'll guarantee they'll listen to reason."

"Mistuh Sheriff," replied the Colonel. "I've listened to my wife heah as she recounted her terrible experiences. While she and my daughter were alone in our cabin it was burned down over their heads. And when they ran out, to save their lives, they were seized by Quick Murrah and his gang. Men like that will do anything—and I know this Quick Murrah for a thorough-paced scoundrel and a murderer. My daughter is in his power, and as long as she remains so I must ask you to stay wheah you are."

"Very well, Colonel," agreed the sheriff after a silence. "But please think this matter over, because I'm satisfied you're making a mistake."

He bowed and turned away and while the posse ate and slept Colonel Blood and his wife sat apart. A great crisis confronted them and the fate of their daughter depended upon the soundness of their judgment, but as the day wore on and the bawling of cattle ceased the Colonel strode down

GUN-SMOKE

towards Gun-smoke. All that morning while the others had tried to talk him over Gun-smoke had kept his post at the edge of the bank with his rifle pushed out to shoot; and even now, when the Colonel settled down beside him, he did not look away from the houses.

"Young man," began the Colonel, "my wife has informed me that you consider Quick's note a blind. Do you think he will make away with Johnsie?"

"I don't know," returned Gun-smoke at last. "But Colonel, I'd feel better if we could slip about twenty men up over that zig-zag trail."

He pointed towards a trail which, mounting up over a high bench, cut down into Portales Canyon, and the Colonel glanced up at it dubiously.

"Don't you reckon," he asked, "that Quick Murrah would see them and——"

"Sure he'd see 'em," admitted Gun-smoke, "but don't you trust him, Colonel. That scoundrel has made up his mind. And if the sun ever sets and those men are not there, you'll never see Johnsie again."

"Why not?" demanded the Colonel, startled.

"Because," said Gun-smoke, "Quick is out for revenge. This is all a bluff about protecting those cattle. He's waiting for the dark, so he can make a night ride—and he'll never give Johnsie up. That half-breed devil is crazy, and the quicker we can kill him the better it will be for—her."

"My God!" exclaimed the Colonel. "But how can we do it?"

"Surround them right now and close in on them at dusk. That's the safest thing to do, in the end. But before we

DIVIDED COUNSEL

start you send your wife back to carry this message to Scorp. You tell him from me that if Johnsie Blood is harmed we'll kill every hound in that house. And I'll take care of him, my ownself."

"By the gods, boy, I'll do it!" cried Colonel Blood, suddenly convinced; and in the midst of a sudden rain Mrs. Blood hurried across the open towards the house where Johnsie was kept. The sheriff, on fire to be up and away before the night closed down, had already assembled his men; but as they stood by their horses awaiting Mrs. Blood's return a mountain storm rolled in upon them. From the black heights of the Culebras it closed down like a shroud, shutting out in quick succession peak and canyon-mouth and town while the posse turned their backs to the rain. But when the storm was at its height, Mrs. Blood came running back and her voice rose sharp and clear.

"She's gone!" she cried. "Scorp says it's too late. Quick took her and rode away when that first rain came. He says they went up the canyon!"

Amidst the drumming of the heavy rain and the cruel lash of the wind the posse stood stunned by the news. But Gun-smoke had jumped his horse out of the wash at her first words and now he turned Watch-eye toward the trail.

"Come on!" he yelled. "We'll cut him off at the Pass." And with a scramble they rode off at his back.

CHAPTER XXII

The End of the Trail

ACROSS the flat and up the trail the posse spurred at a gallop and as they whipped over the bench and started down into Horse-thief Canyon the storm passed as quickly as it had come. The dripping oaks gleamed with raindrops in the setting rays of the sun, muddy water ran roaring down the trail, but when they came out into the pasture not a man or horse was in sight and the posse spread out to cut sign.

Everywhere in the trampled sod were the tracks of thousands of cattle, all pointing towards the northern pass; but every pathway was flooded with a glut of muddy water—Murrah's trail already was washed out.

"Maybe the whelp didn't go!" exclaimed the sheriff as he reined in and looked back towards the houses. "I believe this is just another steer. Zim Plunkett was afraid to give the girl up, so he claimed Quick Murrah had gone."

"I'm going up the canyon to where that trail turns off," said Gun-smoke. "The rain has just washed out his tracks."

"Well, go ahead," assented the sheriff. "But I feel it's my duty to surround that house before dark."

"Nope—Quick's gone," answered Gun-smoke as he turned back up the canyon. "I knew he'd quit the country, but

THE END OF THE TRAIL

by grab I'm going to follow him. So if I don't come back—"
He nodded significantly and Watch-eye took off at a lope.

The flood of water passed away as quickly as it had come, Gun-smoke spied a shod horse-track in the mud; and as he turned up the trampled pathway that led over the mountain he saw two tracks of different size. But further up the trail the dim tracks disappeared again and he spurred on, for night was falling fast. His hand trembled with nervous haste as he reined here and there across the wide path the cattle had left—when darkness closed down Quick Murrah would be safe, and Johnsie Blood would be lost.

In those wild and outlawed mountains there were a hundred paths and trails known only to the rustler band, and Murrah knew them all. He knew the hidden cabins, the secret caves under the rimrock, the rocky trails that topped out over the summit—and all the long night lay before him. For Gun-smoke could not trail him after dark. But as Watch-eye scrambled on the canyon closed in and at a narrow passageway between two boulders he stopped. Jerking impatiently at the bit he craned his neck and snuffed the earth—then he raised his head and neighed.

"What you found?" demanded Gun-smoke, leaping down and running forward. He stooped low, and in the dusk he spied the imprints of a horse-shoe, clear and fresh and made since the rain. Watch-eye raised his head again and his loud, ringing neigh seemed to echo from the mountain heights. Or was it an answering call?

"My God!" breathed Gun-smoke. "That's Star-dust!"

He stood listening, watching the pinto as with ears strained ahead he sought out the answer of his mate. But

GUN-SMOKE

no response came and with a last impatient whicker Watch-eye thrust his nose again to the ground.

"What you smell?" coaxed Gun-smoke. "Is that Billy-boy up there?" And Watch-eye nodded and whinnied softly.

Billy-boy was the name by which he knew his brother, whom Johnsie had renamed Star-dust; and as Gun-smoke still hesitated he bunted him fiercely and took a quick step up the trail.

"Go find him!" directed Gun-smoke, leaping impulsively into the saddle; and Watch-eye went scrambling up and up. His breath was labored now and he grunted when he slipped but at each uplift of the trail he thrust his nose to the ground and whickered as he scented his mate. Gun-smoke sat him lightly now, the better to save his wind, and as the path mounted at last to the broad top of the bench Watch-eye broke into a stumbling trot.

They came out into a broad park, dotted here and there with pines, and with a high, shrill challenge Watch-eye jumped into a lope, rushing forward to the next steep ascent. Straining his eyes into the night Gun-smoke swept the crest ahead and on the knife-blade of the ridge he beheld two riders, mounting up. Watch-eye threw up his head, his neigh sounded again; and at his far-flung call the rear horse set back on his rope. Then, clear and plain, the answer came back, and Gun-smoke gave Watch-eye his head.

It was Star-dust, and the riders seen so dimly against the sky were Johnsie Blood and Murrah. As Watch-eye went bounding up the slope Gun-smoke saw the man look back, then they plunged into the timber and when they

THE END OF THE TRAIL

gained the upper heights Quick Murrah and his captive were gone. But the trail led on and, still whickering expectantly, Watch-eye toiled on from turn to turn. His breathing was broken now for they were far up on the heights and the air was thin and cold, but as they entered another park he broke into a lope, his head high as he stared through the night.

Hour after hour he had alternately watched the sky-line and lowered his nose to sniff the ground; but now, across the park, he halted and looked back and Gun-smoke patted his neck.

"Want to rest?" he asked, stepping swiftly from the saddle and fumbling to loosen the cinch; but Watch-eye smelled the trail and snorted. It was his alarm-call, his signal of danger.

"Now what?" muttered Gun-smoke, "is Quick Murrah trying to bushwack me? My God, old Watch-eye is lost!"

He read the answer plain in the pinto's anxious sniffs as he tested the trails on both sides; then as he stopped and turned back Gun-smoke swung into the saddle and threw the reins on his neck. Like a hound which, hot after a lion, has over-leapt the scent and casts back to pick up the trail; so Watch-eye in tremulous haste followed back on his own tracks, sniffing the ground on both sides as he passed. He stopped short at the very spot where, overcome with eagerness, he had struck into a loping pursuit; then with a deep, explosive snort he turned off to the left, where a trail led down the slope.

"He's found it!" cried Gun-smoke exultantly and reached

GUN-SMOKE

down and patted his neck. Then, nose close to the ground, Watch-eye took up the long pursuit which brought them, just at dawn, upon Quick Murrah.

He had swung back down rocky trails which only a mountain sheep could climb, heading east over ridges and canyon-rims towards some hidden destination, some hold-out in the wilderness of pines. Across mesas and broad parks he had twisted and turned until at last in a narrow canyon set in among the peaks he had fallen into a dim, unused trail. The day was dawning when Gun-smoke broke in after him and saw, clear and fresh in the moist dirt ahead of him, the tracks of two horses, both shod. And Watch-eye, feeling the spurs, broke into a stiff-kneed lope, his nostrils snuffing the wind. Then at a turn of the trail he threw his ears forward and Gun-smoke beheld a valley at their feet. It was small and perfectly round and across its grassy meadow two riders were approaching a house.

Watch-eye raised his head eagerly but as he began a joyous whinny Gun-smoke reached out and caught him by the nose. Then, snatching out his rifle, he dropped to the ground; but the horse in the sunk valley had heard. Just as Gun-smoke, across his sights, beheld the bobbing form of Murrah, Star-dust flung up his head and neighed back. For an instant Quick Murrah sat frozen in his saddle, then he ducked and the bullet missed its mark.

Gun-smoke jacked up another cartridge and threw down on Murrah's horse but before he could pull the trigger Quick reined in behind Johnsie, crouching low, looking up at the trail. In this hidden valley, known only to his men, the attack had come as a surprise; but at sight of Watch-eye

THE END OF THE TRAIL

with his gaudy, pinto hide the source of the bullet was plain. Snatching Johnsie from her saddle he held her close, as a living shield; then, throwing off Star-dust's rope, he rode straight to the house and dropped down behind his horse.

There was a heave and the massive oak door swung open, they passed in and it closed behind them. Gun-smoke threw down his gun and cursed.

CHAPTER XXIII

IN SUNK VALLEY

THE cabin in Sunk Valley was made of stone, a prison and a fort in one. No windows broke its walls, there were not even loop-holes—the only opening was the door. Like a man in a trance Gun-smoke had stood on the hillside and watched Quick Murrah escape; for, struggling in his arms, he held Johnsie Blood and one bullet would have killed them both. But as the door slammed to, cutting off her screams for help, he thrilled to a sudden fear.

Like a gorilla from the forest, carrying off some maiden to his nest in the trackless jungle, Quick Murrah had snatched away Johnsie. All night he had borne her over the trails to this hiding-place; and now, though Gun-smoke had traced him to his hold-out, he had dragged her inside the door. For a moment, staring wildly, Gun-smoke counted the chances of death; then he swung up on Watch-eye and charged.

Down the trail and across the flat they shot like a rocket, Watch-eye running to join his brother after the long night of waiting, Gun-smoke rushing to save Johnsie from her fate. For how could he wait to skirmish and pick ground when her screams still rang in his ears? Even then Quick Murrah might be watching through some loop-hole to pot

IN SUNK VALLEY

him as he charged across the open, but something greater than himself seemed to impel him to instant action and Gun-smoke rode straight for the house.

Throwing the reins on Watch-eye's neck he gave him a slap and ran, crouching low, to the door. But all was quiet inside. Gun-smoke's heart was pounding violently, his breath came in quick gasps; but as he listened he seemed to hear above the blood-pulse in his ears the sound of a half-choked cry.

"Open up!" he ordered, standing to one side of the door and reaching out to give it a kick. "Open the door, before I kill you!"

"Go to hell!" snarled Murrah from within; and as Gun-smoke stepped back two bullets came smashing through the wood.

"I'll git you!" panted Gun-smoke, running swiftly around the house to seek out some loop-hole behind. But back at the door he stopped, and once more in the stillness he heard Jo'insie's gasping sob. He raised his boot again and with a sudden straight kick smashed the lock, leaving the door ajar.

"Git away from thar!" cursed Murrah from the darkened interior. "Damn yore heart, I've got you in the door. And the first move you make to come inside this cabin I'll drill you, through and through!"

Gun-smoke crouched against the wall, his pistol ready to shoot, his eye on the crack of the door. But Quick Murrah did not show his head. Safely hidden in the darkness he had only to wait and Gun-smoke would charge into his guns. But Gun-smoke did not charge.

GUN-SMOKE

"You come out of that!" he said. "I've got a posse behind me. But all we want is Johnsie."

"Heh! That's all I want!" jeered Murrah from his corner. "And by grab, I've got her, too!"

There was the sound of a muffled struggle and Gun-smoke felt his hair rise. Then he jumped in—and slammed the door.

All was dark inside to his sun-dazzled eyes, but as he dodged to one side there was the glare of a pistol-shot from the corner furtherest away from the door. Like a flash he fired back, crouching low against the wall, leaping away from the pistol as it shot; but for all his swiftness a bullet struck his hand, knocking the pistol from his grasp. Even there in the darkness Quick could see him.

Gun-smoke stumbled and with the instinct of a man half-blinded he started back towards the door. He was hit, one gun was missing, and as he groped for the other something told him that here was the end. Quick Murrah was only playing, he had him at his mercy, and the next shot would snuff out his life. But as he faltered he felt an arm suddenly flung around his neck and a soft form pressed against him. It was Johnsie, seeking to protect him from Murrah's bullet.

"Fight! Fight!" she cried in his ear and suddenly sent him whirling as she leapt back and flung open the door. Like a flash of lightning which, splitting the darkness, reveals every detail of the landscape; so the blinding light of morning flooded the darkened interior, and for the first time Gun-smoke saw his enemy. He stood out lean and sinister, his hand on his pistol, his tiger-skin shaps and vest catching the sun, and his strained face was working with hate. Then they drew, both at once, and across the narrow space their gun-flames stabbed like two swords. But Gun-smoke had beat him to it and as if struck by a fist Quick Murrah tumbled backwards—dead.

At last the two fighters had shot out their feud. They had gone for their guns at the first flash of light but Gun-smoke had been quickest on the draw. Murrah's bullet had gone high, clipping a lock from his flying hair, but Gun-smoke stood grimly erect.

"Name's Quick, eh?" he taunted, and turned away laughing to where Johnsie stood staring in the doorway.

"Oh, did you kill him?" she faltered. "Isn't it terrible—the way he looks!" But Gun-smoke was staring at his hand.

"Look at my hand!" he cursed, "if you want to see something terrible! I'll never hold a six-shooter again!"

"Oh, yes, you will," soothed Johnsie, gazing in awe at his mangled fingers. "And if you don't, Gun-smoke," she sobbed, "just think what you did for me! Is that too much—for a finger?"

"Nope! Nope!" grumbled Gun-smoke. "But I'll shore miss 'em, all the same. I'd better get back to a doctor."

"I'll wrap them up for you," she volunteered, leading him out into the sun and glancing up at him with wistful eyes. "Isn't it wonderful for us to be here—alive? And oh, there's Watch-eye, out making friends with Star-dust. How did he follow us, in the dark?"

"The same way," boasted Gun-smoke, "that a hound dog follows a lion! That horse and Star-dust are brothers and he most whinnied his head off when he found your trail, just at dusk. If it wasn't for him I wouldn't've got here."

"But Star-dust was wonderful, too," said Johnsie dotingly as she bandaged up Gun-smoke's hand. "He knew it was Watch-eye and he hung back all night until I thought Quick Murrah would kill him."

"Huh! Watch-eye jumped the trail, up there in that big park where Murrah turned off downhill, and he circled and cut sign like a hound. That's what you might call a real horse!"

"Oh, it's wonderful!" sighed Johnsie. "But I just knew you'd save me. And I'm sorry he hit your hand."

"Oh, that's all right," nodded Gun-smoke. "Doctor'll fix 'em up, I reckon. But say, speaking of this and that being wonderful, how does Mistuh Bill Enright class up?"

"Is that your real name?" she cried ecstatically. "And is Mr. Enright, that brought Star-dust, your father? Then you class up A1, with me!"

"That's good—that's fine," responded Gun-smoke indulgently. "But how was that for shooting, just now? I'm going back to get them shaps and that tiger-skin vest, and wear 'em back to Portales when we go."

"What—off a dead man?" she shuddered. "No, let's—let's just ride away and leave him."

"Not me!" declared Gun-smoke stubbornly. "I took a lot off of Quick Murrah, and I'll just show those Night Riders his shaps. The sheriff and his posse had the house surrounded yesterday and I reckon they've took it, by this time."

"No, don't do it!" she begged. "Because John Murrah is still alive and—and I know he'd shoot you, sure."

"John Murrah?" scoffed Gun-smoke. "I'll kill him left-

IN SUNK VALLEY

handed, the murdering, half-breed rascal. No, I'm going to take them shaps—and I'm going to wear 'em, too. Because if I go back and say I killed Quick your old man will call me a liar again!"

"But if you wear his shaps," she pleaded tearfully, "the posse might think you were Quick Murrah. They'd shoot you if we met them on the trail."

"The girl is right," observed Gun-smoke oracularly. "I reckon my haid ain't working. We'll hang them on his horse and drive him on ahead, like they do at these military funerals."

"But they're unlucky!" cried Johnsie desperately. "I tell you I just hate 'em! Every time I even see 'em I go cold! Oh, Gun-smoke, can't you realize how a woman would feel? Please—please don't take them! Please!"

"Nope!" decided Gun-smoke, "you ain't quite right now, Johnsie. But if I go back without Quick's tiger-skin shaps they won't any of them believe what I done."

"Well, let's go then," assented Johnsie after a silence. "But I know—I just *know*—that something terrible will happen. Only of course you've got to have your own way."

"W'y, sure!" grinned Gun-smoke. "Ain't I just lost two fingers, unless that doctor is better than he looks? Well, gimme my own way, then, like you did that first time, when I thought you were an angel from heaven!"

"Oh, I'm afraid!" sighed Johnsie; but as they rode out of Sunk Valley she reached over and patted Gun-smoke's good hand.

CHAPTER XXIV

THE BELLOWING HERD

GUN-SMOKE had been lost when he left Sunk Valley, for the sun had come up in the north; but as he rode back on his trail and met it in the south he shook his head and glanced at Johnsie.

"Any idea," he enquired, "where Portales is?" And she pointed straight ahead.

"Nope," he said. "That's east—no doubt about it. And I travelled east and north half the night. I reckon you and me are lost."

"Let's go back the way we came," suggested Johnsie. "And then Watch-eye can smell out the trail."

"Too far," objected Gun-smoke. "And old Watch is dead tired. We can't climb over those peaks. But here's this dim trail that Quick cut down into—I believe it leads back to Portales, no matter which way it goes now. Let's turn his horse loose and see what happens!"

"But he might take us the wrong way!" protested Johnsie. "And oh, Gun-smoke, I'm so afraid we'll meet some of Scorp's Night Riders! They'll be hiding, out in these hills. And what if Quick's horse should lead us right back among them!"

"We've got to take a chance," replied Gun-smoke, "or

I'm liable to lose these two fingers. Whole end shot off, now, and——"

"Well, all right!" agreed Johnsie soothingly. "You're so tired you can hardly see, anyhow. But if we find we're lost we must stop and go to sleep. Dad says that's the only way."

"Suits me," mumbled Gun-smoke. "I'm sure dead for sleep. Step up here, horse, and take us back to Portales!" And he turned Quick Murrah's horse loose.

For a moment he stood watching them—then with confident steps he led off down the unused trail.

"Good enough!" observed Gun-smoke. "He's heading for home. All we've got to do is follow his tail."

He fell in behind Quick's mount, and almost immediately Johnsie saw him begin to nod in the saddle. He swayed sidewise, but Watch-eye moved over to check his fall; and soon like a drunken rider he jogged along sound asleep, watched over by his faithful horse. Johnsie smiled, but as the trail led them down into a dark, mysterious canyon she spurred forward and woke Gun-smoke up.

"We're lost!" she cried. "And I—I'm afraid. Let's stop—and then you can sleep."

"Sure! Sure!" agreed Gun-smoke, reining out under some trees. And after tying Quick's mount he stripped the saddle off of Watch-eye and stretched out on the sweaty blankets.

"Go to sleep!" he admonished, his eyes closing in spite of him. "Never mind—old Watch-eye will stand guard."

But Johnsie sat listening, turning quickly at every sound; until at last, creeping over, she took one of Gun-smoke's pistols—the one he might never shoot again. For the right hand beneath its bandages had lost its two middle fingers, shot off by Quick Murrah's bullet. But what if, while they slept, Quick's men should come riding and find them there by the trail! And Quick's horse, and the tiger's-skin shaps! She shuddered and settled down with her eyes on the trail, but the next minute she too was asleep.

The sun mounted higher and Watch-eye who had been drowsing reached down and plucked ravenously at the grass; but as he fed a distant sound made him raise his head and listen, then go on with his satisfied chomping. Star-dust roused up and drifted over to feed beside him, reaching out to snuff and nip at him affectionately; but as the sound down the valley increased and drew nearer Watch-eye snorted, gazing doubtfully at his master. Then, stamping up closer, he breathed into his ear and Gun-smoke woke up with a jerk.

"What's the matter?" he grumbled, sitting up and squinting around; and then on the wind he heard the bellowing of steers and the low, bass rumbling of bulls. "Hell's bells!" he muttered, reaching down for his gun, "what the devil are them cattle doing here? We must be lost, and good and lost, too—plumb over the mountains in Colorado! Because those are Scorp's cows, that he drove over the trail—who else would be moving a herd?"

He rose up stiffly and threw the saddle on his horse; and as Johnsie heard him moving she roused up with a start, then hastened to saddle up Star-dust.

"What is it?" she asked at last.

"Search me!" answered Gun-smoke. "Do you hear them cattle bawling? That's a big, big herd; and they're moving, and moving fast. I'll bet you it's Old Scorp's stuff!"

THE BELLOWING HERD

"Then where *are* we?" cried out Johnsie, bewildered. "They drove them over the mountains—yesterday!"

"That's no lie," nodded Gun-smoke and swung solemnly up on his horse. "We'd better be moving," he said.

Johnsie crouched in the saddle and followed without a word as he led Murrah's mount up the trail, but at a low divide where he could look out the lower country Gun-smoke reined in and rubbed his eyes.

"See that sun?" he asked at last. "Back in the southwest, where it belongs. And them mountains look mighty familiar. Ain't that the big double-peak that lays over west of Portales?"

"Why—why, yes!" agreed Johnsie. "But how did we get here? And what are those cattle doing?"

"You tell me!" answered Gun-smoke. "But I know that double-peak. And if I'm not mistaken that big ridge ahead is the canyon wall west of Portales. Let's ride down and look around!"

"But what if you *are* mistaken," protested Johnsie in a panic, "and we find it's Old Scorp's rustlers?"

"Then they'll kill us," replied Gun-smoke sarcastically, "and I won't have to starve to death. My stomach is shrunk up now until it wouldn't chamber a liver-pill. What I need is a little real nourishment."

He turned back down the trail and Murrah's horse quickened its pace, but Johnsie held back doubtfully. She was hungry, too, but not for all the food in the world would she venture within sight of that herd. She was afraid, but follow she must. Down the long, gloomy canyon they went forward at a trot and at every turn of the trail the bawling

GUN-SMOKE

grew louder until at last they heard the yells of the cowboys. Gun-smoke slowed to a walk as their canyon opened out into the wide, level floor of Horse-thief Canyon; but his hunger had put him in a reckless mood and he rode on until he sighted the herd. It was pouring down the mountain and out into the valley below; and at the point of the herd three men rode with Winchesters while a fourth dragged a reluctant pack animal.

"That's grub," announced Gun-smoke eagerly. "We'll try 'em with Quick Murrah's horse!" And without waiting for Johnsie to make her usual futile protest he slapped him on the rump and sent him flying. If these were the Night Riders, coming back—but Gun-smoke was too ravenous to care.

As the horse with Murrah's shaps burst suddenly into view the three men with Winchesters stepped swiftly to the ground and took shelter behind their mounts. But after a long look at the canyon-mouth from which it had emerged they swung up and headed the horse off. One snatched at the vest, the other grabbed the tiger-skin shaps; then riding at a trot they came back towards the canyon-mouth and Gun-smoke spurred out into the open.

"Who are you?" he yelled, holding up his bandaged hand; and the leader threw up his hand in the peace sign.

"I'm the United States Marshal—from Pueblo!" he answered and Gun-smoke jumped Watch-eye into a lope.

"Then give me some of that grub!" he demanded roughly. "I'm Bill Enright, and I'm danged near dead."

The U. S. Marshal laughed and beckoned up the pack as he rode over and shook hands left-handed.

"I knowed you, boy," he said, "the minute I saw you!

THE BELLOWING HERD

Your Daddy and me used to be pardners back in Dalhart. Name's Billings—I'm shore glad to meet you."

"Never mind the name," grinned Gun-smoke, "as long as you feed me. How'd you happen to be over here, Mr. Billings?"

"The old man wired me from Texmex yesterday to watch Horse-thief Pass for this herd. I met 'em beyond the summit but the rustlers seen me coming. Your Dad said to meet him at Portales."

"Uh-huh—good!" grunted Gun-smoke, dropping down to rustle the pack. "Mr. Billings, I'll make you acquainted with Miss Blood. Git down, Johnsie—here's where we eat!"

He opened a can of tomatoes with two slashes of his big knife-blade and handed it to her gallantly; then, cutting another can, he drained off the contents and greeted his fair partner with a smile.

"Ah!" he sighed, "ain't that the real stuff? Don't that put a little rainbow in the sky? Now kill me a steer, Marshal, and if I don't eat a leg off of him you can have my horse and saddle."

"Done killed him, already!" returned the marshal facetiously, "and saved this quarter for you. Boys, light a fire quick and fry him a big, thick steak. Here's a packbox to sit down on, Miss Blood."

He bowed with great politeness but Gun-smoke took the hint and drew the keen-eyed marshal to one side.

"Don't talk about it," he said, "but Quick Murrah carried her off and I followed the damned scoundrel all night. Came up on him at daylight and there's his vest and shaps. He shot off the ends of my fingers."

GUN-SMOKE

"Bill!" exclaimed the marshal, slapping him heartily on the back, "you're a credit to your Dad, and he was a wolf when it came to gitting his man. Quick as lightning with a six-shooter, too."

"I got Quick left-handed," observed Gun-smoke modestly; and the marshal and his deputies exchanged glances.

"Your father wired me," resumed the marshal as Gun-smoke turned a smoking steak and sat down to eat his share, "that there was a rustler war coming off here shortly. Is that the shooting I hear down below?"

"I haven't heard none," stated Gun-smoke, "on account of them steers bawling; but I reckon it is, all right. Dandy McAllister and the sheriff and about two hundred settlers have got Old Scorp's Night Riders surrounded and they're out to kill the whole gang."

"Well, in that case," remarked the marshal, "while I'm an officer of the law, I believe I'll let Nature take its course. Because Scorp and them Night Riders have sure dealt the settlers misery—boys, we'll hold up the herd, right here!"

He galloped off with his deputies to turn back the drifting cattle and Gun-smoke put on another steak.

"That's my idea of a good officer," he observed to Johnsie. "What say, after we've et, we ride down around the point and see if old Zim has surrendered?"

"No, let's rest!" pleaded Johnsie. "I'm tired."

"Then you rest," suggested Gun-smoke, "and I'll get the news and report, unofficially, to the marshal."

"No, you stay here," coaxed Johnsie, "with me."

"All right," agreed Gun-smoke. "I haven't had so much of your company that I'm liable to hurry away. So you

THE BELLOWING HERD

eat hearty, Johnsie; and after you're plumb rested we'll go down and investigate this shooting."

He cocked his head as a turn of the wind brought the sound of a distant fusillade, then he jumped up and listened intently.

"By grab," he exclaimed, "they're at it, hammer and tongs! Say, you stay here, Johnsie, while I——"

"No—wait!" appealed Johnsie, leaping up from her pack-box, "I—I'm afraid you'll get killed if you go! Something tells me there's danger—the bullets are flying everywhere and—and one of them might hit you!"

"Done hit me, already!" answered Gun-smoke recklessly, holding up his injured hand. "But I can't stay away when there's a fight going on so——"

"Then I'll go with you!" cried Johnsie, impulsively.

"No, but listen!" he protested. "You might get hurt, Johnsie, and——"

"I'm going if you do!" she announced with decision; and Gun-smoke tightened up his cinch.

"All right," he laughed, "there's no danger, anyway!"

But Johnsie shook her head.

"I'm afraid you'll get killed," she repeated.

CHAPTER XXV

THE JONAHED SHAPS

AT the first pop of distant guns Gun-smoke had forgotten his wounded hand. Even his half-satisfied hunger could not hold him. He was drawn toward the conflict as irresistibly as a needle is attracted towards its lode-star in the north. But Johnsie held back and as they came in sight of the battle she reined in and dropped to the ground.

"We're going to stop—right—heah!" she announced and Gun-smoke thrust his tongue into his cheek.

"Since when," he enquired roguishly, "have you took to talking that way? Because I say we're going to go on. Let's ride up on this point, where we can see the fighting!" And with a jab of the spurs he was gone.

"Oh, dear!" sighed Johnsie as she tagged along after him. "He never seems to think of me at all." But as she rode up beside him and saw the battle-field below all her fears and weariness vanished.

A half-circle of men lay dug in around Portales, others shot down from the bench above; and from the stone saloon across the street from Plunkett's house the white smoke rose in a cloud. Answering puffs came now and then from some loop-hole in Scorp's fort, but at every shot a rattle of rapid-fire showed that the posse was pressing them hard.

THE JONAHED SHAPS

"They're whipped," announced Gun-smoke after a few minutes of anxious watching. "Ammunition is running low, I reckon. Now what say, Johnsie, if we ride out in the open and let the sheriff know you're safe? Because we sent word to Plunkett that we'd kill every one of 'em, unless they gave you up."

"Well," agreed Johnsie doubtfully; and once more Gun-smoke moved to the front.

"Eee-whoo!" he yelled, firing two shots into the air to attract the attention of the posse; and as the settlers on the benches saw him riding back with Johnsie they leapt up and gave cheer after cheer.

"You see?" nodded Gun-smoke, "that's how much they think of you. Just wait till I wave these shaps, and Old Scorp will savvy, mighty quick."

"No, please don't!" she begged as he reached over to grab them. "Now listen, or I'm just going to cry. I don't want you to tell them what happened—back there. Can't you see what it meant to me?"

"Sure! Sure!" agreed Gun-smoke repentantly. "I won't say a word—honest, Johnsie! We'll just ride in and you can go to your mother—I reckon she's up here, by now. But I did want 'em to know that you're back, safe and sound. By grab, there's your father, now!"

A tall horseman, closely followed by a pack of hounds came galloping down from the bench; and at sight of her mother's scrubby pony loping behind Johnsie weakened and gave way to tears.

"This is a big day for the folks!" observed Gun-smoke with a smile as neighbors and friends rode to meet them;

and then, his long beard waving, the old Colonel dashed up and gathered Johnsie into his arms.

"My little dove!" he said and Gun-smoke turned away; for the Colonel was crying, too. Then as Mrs. Blood came up and joined in the rejoicing he slipped away and rode towards the front.

"What's all this?" challenged the sheriff, spurring across the flat to meet him. "Did you get her back, safe and sound?"

"Sure did!" answered Gun-smoke. "Ain't Old Scorp surrendered yet? That old rascal must be afraid you'll kill him."

"Certainly is," spoke up a settler, "because we told him so, p'intedly! He knowed all the time what Quick Murrah was up to——"

"Yes, yes!" broke in the sheriff, "but under the circumstances, gentlemen, I believe we'd better show a white flag. I understand Quick Murrah is dead."

He nodded towards the horse which Gun-smoke was leading, with Quick's gun-belt and shaps over the horn; and a few minutes later, when a white flag was raised, another was shown from the house. The firing died down and ceased, and, after a parley across the street, Scorp's Riders began to file out. One by one they came out and laid their guns on the ground in token of unconditional surrender—and then as Old Scorp himself appeared the posse set up a yell.

After years of open violence and defiance of the law Zim Plunkett had been compelled to bow his stubborn neck and acknowledge the settlers' power. Half his Riders had slipped away under cover of the night and those who were left had the hang-dog, spiritless look of men who expect the worst. Only John Murrah, standing by Plunkett, had the hardihood to smile as he faced the vengeful sheriff.

"Well, well!" he mocked, "hyer's our old friend, Hanna. Last time I seen you, you were runnin'!"

"I've come back, young man," answered the sheriff stiffly. "You're my prisoner. And you, Zim Plunkett."

Old Scorp raised his furtive eyes and peered out from under the eye-brows that covered them like an overhanging bush; then looked down, like a fox in a trap. He was caught —his enemies were all around him. But as he glanced up again he saw a man that he knew and his little eyes sparkled with hate. It was Gun-smoke, the boy he had robbed. He rode up regally, still sitting the pinto pony that had leapt over the gate at Portales; and at sight of Plunkett he smiled.

"Howdy, folks! Howdy, Scorp!" he nodded jauntily; and the Night Riders glared back at him hatefully.

"Well, laff!" snarled Scorp at last as his anger boiled over. "You think you're so smart, riding that pinto hawse around! Go ahead and laff, you danged idjit!"

"All right, Uncle," retorted Gun-smoke. "You thought *you* were smart, too, when you held me up at that gate. If you'd let me pass through you wouldn't be here now, with a bunch of deputy sheriffs on your neck."

"I don't want nothing to do with you!" yapped Scorp, swelling with venom. "You danged, swelled-up kid, I shore wish I'd killed you when I seen you coming down the road!"

"Well, you tried!" taunted Gun-smoke. "Only I was a little too swift for you and this lousy bunch of horse-thieves you've got here. You thought you'd play hell, didn't you—

holding me up for the drinks, and then ribbing up a horse-race? But when you held out my money you done pulled the house down on you, because I don't let no man rob me. Just for that I went back and bought up all those notes—and Mistuh Enright, that you thought was only a cattle-buyer, was my own Dad, all the time. We certainly trimmed you good."

"You cheated me!" accused Plunkett. "You robbed me of my steer-money. But I'll git you—I ain't done, yet!"

"All right," agreed Gun-smoke. "You go ahead and try it. And that goes for the rest of you yaps. I just thought I'd ride over and take a good look at you, so I'd know you, next time we meet."

"We'll meet!" spoke up John Murrah and Gun-smoke glanced at him knowingly; then he nodded his head and smiled.

"Any time," he said. "I'll sure be looking for you. But if you figure on selling those cattle and hiring some blackleg lawyer to keep you and your gang out of the pen—you'll have to guess again, Mr. Murrah."

"What cattle?" demanded Murrah, arrogantly.

"That herd you sent ahead, over the divide. Because the United States Marshal met your rustler friends in the pass and he's bringing every hoof of them back."

Murrah blenched and stepped back and the other Riders exchanged glances, but Scorp Plunkett burst out cursing.

"You're a dadrammed liar!" he yelled.

"Oh, I am, eh?" answered Gun-smoke. "You hear that noise up the canyon? That's your herd, you danged old cow-thief!"

THE JONAHED SHAPS

He paused and as every ear was strained there came the sound of the great herd, lowing. But in the silence that had fallen Gun-smoke heard his own name spoken and turned to find Johnsie at his side. Her face was tense and drawn and as she reined Star-dust closer she whispered anxiously into his ear.

"Look out!" she warned, "John Murrah is fixing to kill you. I can tell by the look in his eye."

She glanced at Murrah as she spoke and he flashed back a look of hate, but Gun-smoke was playing a game of his own.

"W'y, of course he is!" he said, speaking out loud. "Don't I know he's fixing to kill me? I can tell by that mean, snaky look in his eye—and so I'm waiting right here, to accommodate him. He's got a gun hid, under his arm."

He paused and John Murrah met his eyes with a steely glare, but he did not reach for the gun.

"You folks get away, behind him," warned Gun-smoke. "Because when he goes for that gun, I shoot. But the cowardly half-Injun is just like Ed and Quick—he's afraid to give a man an even break."

"Now here, gentlemen!" spoke up the sheriff, stepping forward officiously and throwing his gun on Murrah, "this man is my prisoner and I'm responsible for his safe-keeping, but we'll find out first of all if he's armed. Search him well!" he said to his deputies.

Murrah stepped back defiantly, with the panther-like swiftness which had made Quick such a terror to the officers; but as the sheriff cocked his gun and presented it at his heart he put up his hands and smiled.

GUN-SMOKE

"Another time!" he said; and Gun-smoke regarded him grimly.

"You're just like Quick," he sneered. "I've been watching you for five minutes, and you were afraid to go for your gun. If you'd've made a crooked move I'd've sent you to hell after him—there's his gun-belt and shaps, on yon horse!"

"Where?" demanded Murrah, and as Gun-smoke turned to point every eye, except one, followed his glance. Johnsie Blood was watching Murrah, and in her lap across the saddle she held Gun-smoke's big, right-hand gun.

Murrah looked with lightning swiftness, then as the sheriff followed suit he reached out and plucked his pistol from its scabbard.

"Take that, you——" he hissed and swung the gun towards Gun-smoke's broad back. But before he could pull the trigger Johnsie Blood shot him twice and fell in a faint from her horse.

John Murrah lurched forward, firing his pistol into the air; and when Gun-smoke whirled he saw his enemy lying dead and Johnsie, pale as death, on the ground. The feud was over and in that brief instant the last of the Murrahs had died.

There was a rush of people to help. Johnsie was carried to her mother; but Gun-smoke sat his horse in a trance. Then as he glanced at Quick Murrah's mount and saw the tiger-skin shaps he remembered Johnsie's warnings.

"Here!" he said, as they bore John Murrah off, "take these shaps and bury them with him. Because Johnsie was right—they're Jonahed!"

CHAPTER XXVI

THE WET DOG

WHILE deputy sheriffs and settlers trampled past his bed Gun-smoke slept the clock around on the floor of the saloon and woke up to find his father bending over him.

"Wake up!" he said, "and let this doctor see those fingers. I brought him clear out from Texmex."

"Lemme sleep," grumbled Gun-smoke. "What time is it?"

"Ten o'clock—and day-after-tomorrow," answered Enright. "Git up and hear the little birdies sing."

Gun-smoke rose up reluctantly and held out his hand, but the doctor after removing the bloody bandages only shook his head and grunted.

"What about it?" demanded Enright anxiously. "Will he lose the use of his hand?"

"Hell—no!" replied the doctor. "But at the same time, Bill, it won't be quite so good for shooting. Lost the first joints of these two middle fingers, and the whole hand is spattered with lead."

"Well, you fix it up!" ordered Enright, "and I'll give you a thousand dollars, cash. I hope, William," he went on, addressing his son, "this affair has been a lesson to you."

"Sure has!" grinned Gun-smoke. "If I hadn't practiced shooting left-handed, Quick Murrah would've got me, for a certainty."

GUN-SMOKE

"Now here!" admonished Enright, "don't you talk back to your father. You know as well as I do that you've been running hog-wild—biggest wonder in the world you ain't been killed. But the time is past for this permiscuous fighting and shooting, and taking on feuds with rustlers. If it hadn't been for that girl, John Murrah would have bored you through and through."

"That's right," agreed Gun-smoke, after a silence. "By grab, she's shore a fighting Blood! And fainted dead away, she was that wore out and weak. We'll have to do something for Johnsie."

"And the Colonel," added his father significantly. "Fix that hand up, Doc—I'll be back again, shortly."

He hurried away and after an unpleasant half hour Gun-smoke met him coming back.

"Now here, son," he said, beckoning Gun-smoke into a corner where they could sit down cross-legged in the shade, "I'm going to need a little help from you. So if you can get your mind off of this shooting and killing we'll talk business a while, for a change. This is a fine cattle country—good grass, and protected from blizzards. How'd you like to settle down here a while? Well, all right, now here's what I'll do."

He picked up a stick and traced cow-brands in the dust as he sketched out the details of his plan, then he threw it away and summed the matter up.

"Now here's the way we're fixed—I've made arrangements with Hanna to hold all those stolen cattle while he looks up the owners. But at the same time Zim Plunkett has got a lot of straight ZIPs that can't be taken away from

THE WET DOG

him. So I've made another trade to take over his brand and remnant, and buy out his rights in this canyon. Old Scorp shore hates me, but he feels the need of some ready cash to hire him a high-class lawyer."

"He'll need one," commented Gun-smoke. "And then what?"

"I see," observed Enright, "you're still thinking about that girl—and by the way, she's gone back to Blood's Canyon. Yes, the Colonel is going back to build him a new home in place of the one that was burned—and that brings me down to the point. We're under obligations of different kinds to the Colonel and his good wife and daughter. Very special obligations, you'll admit, but they can't be paid for with money."

"Ump-umm!" spoke up Gun-smoke. "He won't take a dollar. I tried it one time, and I know."

"At the same time," continued his father, "there's a way to do everything. And, for services rendered in the buying up of Zim's notes, I've decided to reimburse Colonel Blood the full amount on his own. You gave him ten per cent—now put up a big talk and get him to accept the balance. It'll be eighteen thousand dollars in all, and I'll pay it in cattle or cash."

"Make it cattle," suggested Gun-smoke, "and I'll kinder look after them." And Enright regarded him knowingly.

"Son," he said, "I'll tell you what I'll do. You trade the old Colonel out of that daughter of his and I'll stake you to ten thousand cows."

"I'll do it for nothing!" came back Gun-smoke enthusiastically. "Ain't she the finest little lady you ever saw?"

"She reminds me of your mother," observed his father quietly. "And by the way, Bill, I promised her something. I told her if we came through this rustler war alive we'd settle down and be home-folks again. No shooting—is that a go?"

"Suits me," agreed Gun-smoke. "These fingers hurt like hell. Believe I'll ride down and say 'Howdy' to Johnsie."

He rose to his feet and stretched but Enright interposed a veto.

"You stay here," he ordered, "for one week. Did you hear what I'm paying that doctor?"

"No, but listen," pleaded Gun-smoke. "I never thanked Johnsie for what she did to John Murrah."

"No, and don't you never do it," advised his father earnestly. "Don't you mention him, in any way. You talk about the sunshine and the birdies in the trees and Johnsie will treat you fine. But you'd better stay away a few days."

"Can't do it!" protested Gun-smoke. "But I'll tell you what I will do—I'll wait till tomorrow morning."

"I reckon you will," promised Enright, "after what I'll say to that doctor! But all right—you can go in the morning."

He slapped him on the back approvingly and the next morning at dawn Gun-smoke hit the trail to the south. Watch-eye bowed his neck and squealed at the prod-prod of the spurs; then, bucking stiff-legged, he fell into a long lope and Gun-smoke burst into a song. The world looked good, but as he approached Blood's Canyon a shadow came over his thoughts. What words could he use in asking that great question? And how would Johnsie answer him?

THE WET DOG

"I'll see the Colonel first," he decided at last, but even then new difficulties arose. For if, at the gift of a horse, Colonel Blood had ordered him off; what would he say at the offer of real money? The more he studied on the matter the more it became apparent that the Colonel would never accept and in that case he would forbid him the ranch.

"No, I'd better see Johnsie!" he said; but Watch-eye, who had been listening, shook his head.

"Aw, what do you know about it?" demanded Gun-smoke. "You wait till you're spoken to, Mistuh Horse! But at the same time," he went on, "I believe old Watch is right. Got to square myself, somehow, with the Colonel!"

He spread his arms like a flying bird and leaned forward in the saddle and Watch-eye took the curves like a flash; but as they came to the Blood gate and leapt the bars on the run Gun-smoke jerked his horse to a halt. A big gang of workmen was erecting a new house, much bigger than the cabin that had been burned; and in a tent under the trees he glimpsed the Colonel himself, sitting in state with a bottle in front of him. And across the table sat Dandy McAllister, a box of cigars in his hand.

"Ex-cuse—me!" murmured Gun-smoke, reining quietly away. "I'm about as welcome here as a wet dog at a picnic. Hell's bells—Dandy's trying to steal my girl!"

CHAPTER XXVII

The Judgment of Watch-eye

GUN-SMOKE'S castle of dreams had been fetched tumbling about his ears by the familiar picture he had seen—the Colonel, drinking whisky; Dandy McAllister with the cigars; and the workmen building a new, frame house. While he had been lying asleep the master of Barcee had restored himself to grace. For the Colonel had lost all his worldly possessions in the fire which had destroyed his poor home, and to whom else could he turn in his extremity except this suitor for his daughter's hand? It was a picture which explained itself and Gun-smoke spurred his horse savagely as he swung back to escape being seen.

"Come on!" he cursed as Watch-eye fought the bit and turned his eager eyes up the canyon; but the pinto had caught the scent of Star-dust on the wind and he raised his head and neighed shrilly. Gun-smoke ducked and worked his spurs as from far up the canyon there came an answering neigh; and then at a high lope Star-dust rounded the point, with Johnsie jerking the bit. Her hair was flying wildly as she dashed past the house; and when, behind the hill, she came up with Gun-smoke her dark eyes were snapping mad.

THE JUDGMENT OF WATCH-EYE

"Now you quit that!" she cried, giving Star-dust a futile kick; but already he was nose-to-nose with Watch-eye.

"Excuse me," murmured Gun-smoke, "I was just making a swift sneak when——"

"Oh, you don't need to explain!" cried Johnsie in a rage. "I know just what you think! But I'm never going back, as long as Dandy is there—the idea of him getting Daddy drunk!"

"Well, come on, then," proposed Gun-smoke, "and let's get out of this before the Colonel sees my horse. Because the way things are breaking he's liable to take a shot at me or——"

"Let's run away!" challenged Johnsie as she put her horse to the gate. "Let's ride clear out on the plains. I feel so shut up in that narrow little canyon, I declare I'm like to bust."

"Beat you over!" yelped Gun-smoke, heading Watch-eye for the fence; and with a strong, sure bound he cleared the sticks and went galloping out across the plains. It was glorious and as Johnsie reined in beside him her eyes were glowing with joy. As free as two children they loped far out on the prairie, stopping for dinner at a homesteader's hut; and Gun-smoke, remembering his father's advice, spoke of nothing but sunshine and life.

The prairie-dogs sat up to watch them gallop past, their little paws hanging slack on their stomachs; eagles circled the blue sky, blue-jays squawked from the thickets and the ground-owls bowed solemnly from their mounds. A jack-rabbit bounded up and led them a chase that soon left them far behind; and then on a grassy knoll they sat and watched the sun as it sank lower and lower towards the peaks. All the world seemed very beautiful.

Johnsie smoothed down her tangled hair and the rebellious light left her eyes as she gazed out over the boundless plain. For a thousand level miles it led on, and everywhere there were covered wagons and new homes. But to the west, beneath the sun which was swinging towards its rest, the great mountains rose, blue and dreamlike. She sighed and rose up, reluctantly.

"Where are we?" she asked, smiling maliciously. "Oh, you bad boy, what will Daddy say now?"

"Done warned me away already," answered Gun-smoke. "We're plumb the other side of Barcee."

"Let's go home some other way," she said. "I wonder if Dandy is still waiting?"

"More'n likely," opined Gun-smoke. "But there's one day I stole from him. He doesn't even know where you've gone."

"Let's ride back through Barcee, then," proposed Johnsie mischievously, "and his Mexicans will see us and tell him. I'll bet he'll be hopping mad."

"All right!" agreed Gun-smoke, whistling for Watch-eye and Star-dust; and soon they were riding into town. But it was not the old Barcee—already on the townsite the new houses were rising like mushrooms. Peace had come, and the railroad was near. Busy carpenters looked up to wave a hand as they passed and the children ran out to stare, for the big man on the pinto with the glassy white eyes was Gun-smoke, who had killed Quick Murrah. But Johnsie had lost her smile, for under the big trees ahead lay the Casa Grande, where she still might be queen.

"Oh, let's not ride by it!" she spoke up impulsively as they approached the ancient house. "Let's cut through here and cross the creek at the ford. I—I don't want to meet him, now."

Gun-smoke shrugged his shoulders and swung down the lane that led to the old Indian crossing, which had been used before the bridge was built. No one passed that way now except Mexicans on horseback and stray settlers riding to the store, but as they circled the broad plaza and came out among the cottonwoods they met Juan Brabon, hurrying home. For a moment he stood gaping, as stiff and frozen as on the day when he had eaten the stones; then his ragged hat came off and he bowed to them both, but with a strange, frightened look in his eyes.

"*Kai, Come-piedras!*" greeted Gun-smoke as they passed; but when he glanced back he was gone. Only the tail of his loose shirt, flapping wildly as he fled, told of the panic which their presence had caused.

"Juan must've seen a ghost," observed Gun-smoke; but Johnsie had not deigned him a glance. He was the father of Lolita, the dancer.

"Come on!" she whispered anxiously and spurred her horse toward the ford, where the brawling brook dashed over the rocks. But her haste was her undoing for as they glanced up the creek-bed she beheld the very man she sought to avoid. He was walking away from them up a path among the willows, and by his side tripped Lolita, her lips parted in a smile as she gazed up into his laughter-lit eyes. It was a very pretty picture but Johnsie turned deathly pale and plunged her horse across the shallow ford. Then Gun-smoke,

GUN-SMOKE

looking back, saw Dandy's arm around the waist of this woman who loved him too well. And on the bank stood the Stone-eater, staring.

In a hard, steady lope, Johnsie led all the way until they came to the mouth of the canyon; but at the gate she stopped and stood irresolute, for she feared to face her father. Dusk was falling, the day was done; and now at the end the old bitterness came back into her heart.

"Won't you come in?" she asked perfunctorily as Gun-smoke let down the bars; but he shook his head and turned away.

"I'll be going," he said, picking up Watch-eye's rein; but suddenly her manner changed.

"No—don't go!" she urged. "I—I'm afraid to go in and—oh, how I hate it, this miserable pretense that Dandy and I are still friends! Did you see him there, with that woman?"

"Sure did," nodded Gun-smoke glumly.

"After coming up heah!" she raged. "And being so nice to Dad! And lending him more money—on nothing! And all the time telling how he loves me!"

She stamped her foot, but Gun-smoke did not speak until Johnsie bowed her head against the bars.

"Say, listen, Johnsie," he pleaded, "why won't you let me help you? I came down here this morning to talk business with your father—he don't need to borrow money from Dandy. But I can't do a thing as long as he's drinking and——"

"Yes, and whose fault is it?" she railed, "that he drinks all the time? Oh, I just hate that Dandy McAllister! He does it on purpose, so I'll have to be nice to him because

THE JUDGMENT OF WATCH-EYE

we can't pay our bill at the store. But you wait till he comes back and I'll tell him a few things that will make his ears burn for a week!"

"Now here," spoke up Gun-smoke, "what's the use of being peoned to that store? Do you want to get out of this hole? Then all you've got to do is to listen to reason, because I'm sure going to give you the chance. My old man sent me down here to notify your father that, for services rendered in trimming Old Scorp, he was going to pay for those notes in full. So there's eighteen thousand dollars that your father can have by just reaching out his hand."

"We don't accept charity!" exclaimed Johnsie haughtily. "And just because we're poor——"

"Never mind, now," broke in Gun-smoke, "I know just what you're going to say. I swear you Southerners are all the same. You won't accept money that you've earned ten times over. You're too proud to work—and you're too proud to pay your debts. All you want is to run up a bill at some store—owned of course, by a 'gentleman', like McAllister!"

"You're worse than a Southerner!" came back Johnsie angrily. "You're nothing but a lowdown Texican! But I'll give you to understand that the Bloods are Virginians—and the Culpepers are Virginians, too!"

"All right," answered Gun-smoke, "I see there's no use talking. Because when you folks get to blowing about your family the King of England is a two-spot. But just to put your mind at rest about Texas my old man is from Indiana, like Sam Bass. And believe me, when he arrived, he made them Texans step around some—he showed 'em that a Northerner can shoot. But come on, Watch-eye, we done wore out our welcome, so we'll hit the trail for Portales."

He slapped the rein over his neck, but when he pulled Watch-eye away he shook his head and turned back to Star-dust.

"What's that you say?" demanded Gun-smoke, holding his ear down and pretending to listen, "you don't want to go and leave Billy-boy? But he don't belong to us, now, boy—I done traded him to Johnsie for a kiss!"

He ran his hand up Watch-eye's neck, and as it neared his ears Watch-eye snorted and shook his head.

"Well, I did!" declared Gun-smoke. "Only by grab, now you mention it, I don't recollect being paid!"

He glanced back at Johnsie, who was watching him half-smiling; but she sighed and gave Star-dust a pat.

"Then good-bye, Pet," she said, "because a Blood from Virginia doesn't swap for her horses like a No'therner. You can take back your horse, Mistuh Enright—I don't trade kisses, at all."

"All right," grumbled Gun-smoke, "if you think you're too good for me. But at the same time, Johnsie, I'd sure take it mighty kind——"

"We'll leave it to Watch-eye!" broke in Johnsie, throwing her arm around the pinto's neck and putting one foot on his hoof.

"Now, Watch-eye," she began, "you're a gentleman, aren't you? And you understand women, too—in fact, you're a regular ladies' horse. But don't you think now that Mistuh Gun-smoke is taking an unfair advantage of a lady?"

She gave him a little jab above his hoof and Watch-eye nodded violently.

THE JUDGMENT OF WATCH-EYE

"Now, you see?" she teased, "your old horse has turned against you—and he didn't bite me, either!"

"Hey, you leave that horse alone!" ordered Gun-smoke peremptorily. "You've spoiled him—you been giving him sugar. I may be a bum, but I've got *some* rights. And Watch-eye'll never quit me—will you Watch?"

He reached up to tickle his ears, but there on his neck he encountered another hand. It was Johnsie's and she let him hold it.

"Oh, what's the use of quarrelling?" she sighed at last. "Don't you think we'd better forgive him, Watch-eye?"

Their hands crept up together and Watch-eye nodded perfunctorily as they lingered in a final caress. Then Johnsie slipped under his neck and gave Gun-smoke a swift kiss before she went dancing away.

"That's to pay you for Star-dust," she called back mockingly. "There's your trade-kiss, you horse-stealing Texican. And heah," she laughed, turning to slip into his arms, "is one that I *give* you, my ownself!"

Dane Coolidge was born in Natick, Massachusetts. He moved early to northern California with his family and was graduated from Stanford University in 1898. In his summers he worked as a field collector and in 1896 was employed by the British Museum in this capacity in northern Mexico. Coolidge's background as a naturalist is a trade mark in his Western fiction along with his personal familiarity with the vast, isolated regions of the American West and its deserts — especially Death Valley. Coolidge married Mary Roberts, a feminist and professor of sociology at Mills College, in 1906. In the summers, these two ventured among the Indian nations and together they co-authored non-fiction books about the Navajos and the Seris. *Hidden Water* (1910), Coolidge's first Western novel, marked the beginning of a career that saw many of his novels serialized in magazines prior to book publication. There is an extraordinary breadth in these novels from *Wunpost* (1920) set in Death Valley, to *The Fighting Danites* (1934) focusing on the early Mormon period in Utah, to *Maverick Makers* (1931), a Texas Rangers story. Many of his novels are concerned with prospecting and mining, from *Shadow Mountain* (1920) and *Lost Wagons* (1923) based on actual historical episodes in the mining history of Death Valley, to a fictional treatment of Colonel Bill Greene's discovery of the fabulous Capote copper mine in Mexico, a central theme in *Wolf's Candle* (1935) and *Rawhide Johnny* (1936). *The New York Times Book Review* commented on *Hell's Hip Pocket* (1939) that "no other man in the field today writes better Western tales than Dane Coolidge." Coolidge, who died in 1940, wrote with a definite grace and leisurely pace all but lost to the Western story after the Second World War although Nelson Nye, an admirer and friend of Coolidge's, tried in his own fiction to capture this same ambiance. Coolidge's stories are set over a period of years and possess a charming sense of *temps en passant*, a visual sensation in which believable characters pass in and out of the narrative, events happen, time passes, but the permanent frame is always the land itself. Such attention to authenticity makes a Dane Coolidge Western story rewarding to readers of any generation.

```
W    98993 15.95
Coolidge, Dane.
GUN-SMOKE.
```

[OTHER BORROWERS WILL APPRECIATE THE PROMPT RETURN OF THIS BOOK]

DEMCO

MADISON-JEFFERSON COUNTY PUBLIC LIBRARY